Praise for *T[...]*

"In his powerfully evoked debut, Roers por[...] experiences that shape the lives of two brothers, Michael and Ron Dougherty, and their friend Ricky Stedman, during the late 1940s in Minneapolis.... Roers shows great skill at maintaining the momentum of his storytelling and the tension between his characters. Through smooth prose, a splash of humor and concise but effective details, he sweeps the reader onto empathetic, emotional white water, joining these sensitively portrayed characters as they cascade from youthful insouciance to rage, pity and remorse."

–Publishers Weekly

"*The Pact*, a first novel by Walter Roers, is a stunner. It is, at once, a gentle and ferocious tale, a coming-of-age story that is most likely an autobiographical novel. Set in the late 1940s in Minnesota, *The Pact* is about a friendship between two pre-teen lads. Their intense bonding is heightened by their shared secrets, each coming from what has become known as a dysfunctional family.... This is a story that will haunt you."

–David Rothenberg, WBAI/FM, NYC

"... Roers has sympathy for all his characters, and there is beauty in his descriptions of life in those sweetly innocent years just after World War II. The author ... suffuses his story with details that everyone who came of age in those years will remember."

–Mary Ann Grossmann, *St. Paul Pioneer Press*

the Pact

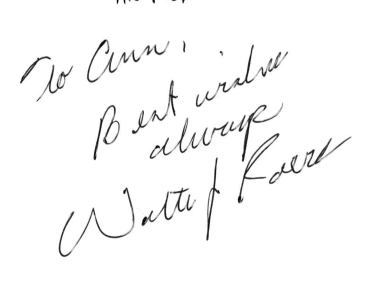

To Ann,
B est wishes
always

Walter F. Roark

the Pact

A Novel

WALTER J. ROERS

Minnesota Voices Project Number 98

New Rivers Press

2000

Cover photograph courtesy the Minnesota Historical
Society; reproduced by permission.

New Rivers Press is a nonprofit literary press dedicated to publishing emerging writers.

The publication of *The Pact* has been made possible by generous grants from the Elmer L. and Eleanor J. Andersen Foundation, the Jerome Foundation, and the Target Foundation on behalf of Dayton's, Mervyn's California, and Target Stores.

This activity is made possible in part by a grant provided by the Minnesota State Arts Board, through an appropriation by the Minnesota State Legislature. In addition, this activity is supported in part by a grant from the National Endowment for the Arts.

Additional support has been provided by the General Mills Foundation, the McKnight Foundation, the Star Tribune Foundation, and the contributing members of New Rivers Press.

NATIONAL
ENDOWMENT
FOR THE
ARTS

MINNESOTA
STATE ARTS BOARD

New Rivers Press
MSUM
1104 7th Avenue South
Moorhead, MN 56563

www.newriverspress.com

There was a time when meadow, grove, and stream,
The earth, and every common sight,
To me did seem
Appareled in celestial light,
The glory and the freshness of a dream.
It is not now as it hath been of yore; —
Turn whereso'er I may,
By night or day,
The things which I have seen I now can see no more.

—William Wordsworth

To Christina

One

The building where we lived is gone now, simply swept aside to make room for a freeway. It stood on the corner of Eighteenth Street and Elliot Avenue in south Minneapolis, a five-story building made of brick the color of dried blood. We lived in one of the two basement apartments—the one that faced east, the Elliot Avenue side of the building. There were five of us cramped into a tiny, one-bedroom unit: my parents, my older brother, Ron, my younger sister, Katy, and me. I suppose it could be argued that we lived in a state of relative poverty, but it was a time when children weren't so acutely aware of how the rest of the world lived, a time when children felt less pressured to be sophisticated and cynical beyond their years.

My world, at the age of eight, was small geographically and devoid of nearly all luxuries, but seemed to me to lack nothing in the way of excitement, mystery, and adventure. My friends and I managed to fill our days with those critical and frivolous activities of childhood, without the slightest suspicion of being deprived in any way.

After saying this, I must quickly add that there was also a darker side to this less complex period. As in any time, you grew to recognize the fallibility and torment of adults and authorities in your life. Sometimes the understanding came slowly, as with the terrible struggle and agonies of my father. At other times, it came swiftly and with a paralyzing shock that unalterably changed your view of life, as with the horrible secret of Ricky Stedman and his mother.

I first met Ricky on a warm, windless Tuesday in June of 1948. Ron and I were on our way to Rodriguez's drugstore, which for some forgotten reason we always pronounced "Rotograph's." It was located on the southwest corner of our block and faced the wide, heavily trafficked street of Chicago Avenue. To get to Rotograph's we had only to walk the short half-block from Elliot to Chicago, across the alley and past Leo's Ice House.

Ron and I always walked fast on our way to the drugstore, in the hope of avoiding any conversation with Leo. It wasn't that we feared or disliked Leo; we simply didn't like being delayed by his dull, rambling questions, and his odd laughter at our answers.

"He's out there," Ron said. "Just keep walking fast. I think maybe he's sleeping."

I nodded in agreement.

"Don't look at him."

I kept pace with Ron and, without moving my head in Leo's direction, glanced only with my eyes as we approached the front of the ice house.

Leo was sitting on a wooden chair that was propped against the front of his shed. Only the back legs of the chair touched the ground. His arms were folded across his chest and his head was slumped forward so that his chin looked like it grew out of the bottom of his throat. The ice house was really no more than a wooden shack made of unfinished planks weathered to a dusty gray. It always looked to me like a miniature house without windows, made of ashes. Above the small entryway was a hand-painted sign that spelled out "Ice House" in wobbly letters.

The slumbering Leo suddenly came to life, leaned forward, and brought his chair to rest on all four legs. "Good morning, boys," he said. He worked his large tan hands back and forth along the tops of his thighs. "Where you two going?"

Being the oldest, Ron always represented both of us to any inquiring adults. "Me and my brother are just going over to Rotograph's."

Leo's large head bowed slightly, and we could hear the familiar chuckle rattle around in his throat. He reached up with one hand and rubbed his woolly gray hair. Finally, he raised his head and looked at us, squinting into the sun so that his eyes were shadowy folds in his round, weathered face. "How are your folks?"

"Fine, sir. Just fine," Ron said.

"They still having their ice delivered?"

Ron shifted his weight from one foot to the other. "Yes sir."

"They could get it cheaper here, you know. Why, two big fellows like you could haul it in your wagon. You have a wagon, don't you?"

"He knows we do," I whispered to Ron. Ron reached back and gave my arm a just-keep-quiet squeeze.

"Yes sir," Ron said.

"You should talk to your folks about that. Tell them old Leo can save them some money. They could keep their icebox cold for a week at half the price. Tell them you could haul the ice in your wagon."

"I'll tell them," Ron quickly replied. "Me and my brother really have to go now. My mom wants us home right away, we got some stuff we have to do for her," he lied.

Leo was not about to let the conversation end. "How old are you boys now?" he asked, as if Ron had made no mention of our need to hurry.

"I'm twelve and Mike is eight," Ron said. "We really got to go now. Nice talking to you, sir."

Leo laughed his little throaty laugh and started to speak again, but Ron just turned away and pulled me by the elbow. "So long sir," he shouted as he ushered me along toward the drugstore.

As we neared the corner, safely out of Leo's sight, we saw a boy about my size standing alone in front of Rotograph's. He had carrot-colored hair that was cut short and even, perhaps within a quarter inch of his scalp. His pale blue eyes watched us with a steady but frightened look as we approached, almost as if he were afraid not to watch us. He wore khaki shorts that were too large for him and gave his thin legs a scrawny, sickly appearance. A clean red-and-white striped T-shirt was tucked into his shorts.

"Hiya kid," Ron said.

"Hi."

"You live around here?" Ron asked.

"Yeah," the boy said and looked at the ground. "We just moved in."

"Where?"

"Over there," the boy said without looking up, and pointed in the direction of our building.

"Where over there?" Ron said in his most nonthreatening voice.

"Across from the big red building."

"Oh, yeah?" Ron said. "You live right across the street from us."

"Uh-huh," the carrot-haired boy said, as if he had known this fact from the start.

"What's your name?"

Carrot-hair looked up at my brother. "Ricky. Ricky Stedman."

"Hi, Ricky," my brother said. "I'm Ron Dougherty and this is my brother, Mike."

Ricky Stedman looked directly at me for the first time. "Hi, Mike," he said in a sort of monotone voice.

"Hi." I followed with my most important question. "What grade are you in?"

"Going into third."

"Me too. Maybe we'll be in the same class. You'll be going to Madison School, right?"

"I guess so."

At this point Ron must have decided that my conversation was leading nowhere and that he needed to redirect things. "Mike and me are going into Rotograph's to get suicide Cokes," he said. "Do you know what a suicide Coke is?"

Ricky Stedman shook his head.

"It's one squirt of every flavor at the fountain, mixed with Coke. Old Rotograph makes the best suicide Cokes in town. Come on with us and have one."

"Can't," Ricky said as he stared at the sidewalk.

"It's okay if you haven't got any money," Ron said. "We can get an extra straw."

"Can't go in. I have to wait here for my mom."

"Well, where's your mom?" Ron said.

"She's in the drugstore, and I have to wait here for her."

While Ron was obviously trying to think of some way to react to this odd piece of information, a streetcar clattered past us. It was headed north on Chicago Avenue toward downtown. The metal wheels of the yellow wooden car clacked and screeched along the steel tracks, giving Ron an extra moment to reflect on Ricky Stedman's situation.

Suddenly, Ron smiled and dug deep into the pocket of his jeans. "Ricky, you see this penny?"

"Yeah."

"Bet I can make it big as a quarter. Have you ever seen a penny as big as a quarter?"

"Nope."

I knew what Ron had in mind. If you put a BB on the streetcar track, it would flatten out as big as a dime when the car rolled over it. A penny could be crushed in an instant to the size of a quarter.

"Watch this, Ricky. I'm going to make this penny as big as a quarter."

Just as Ron finished promising this incredible trick, a woman's voice, loud and demanding, came from behind us. Ricky winced, as though the sound had struck him with physical force. "Get over here, Ricky—this instant!"

Ron and I turned toward the voice to see a woman of astounding height. She was thin and not particularly pretty, and the scowl on her face made me think of the word mean. But, more than her height or her forceful voice or her scowl, what made the greatest impression on me were her eyes. They seemed to have no color, just tiny black dots lost in a murky pool of white and gray. I couldn't stop looking at her eyes, though I wanted to look away, to not be seen by her.

"Right now, Ricky!"

Our new acquaintance marched dutifully to her side. The woman reached down and grabbed Ricky by the hand. She turned quickly and mechanically marched away with Ricky in tow.

Ron and I watched as Ricky's scrawny little legs tried to keep up with the woman's long, rapid stride. I heard her say something about staying away from "boys like that." Then, just as I was about to turn away, I saw Ricky Stedman look back at Ron and me, and with his free hand he gave us a little good-bye wave.

Two

Wednesday night was Dish-Night at the Franklin Theater. Every adult who went to the movie got a free dish or kitchen utensil of some kind. Before Katy was born, Mom and Ron and I went maybe four or five times to the movies on Dish-Night. It was a great way to spend an evening, especially if there was enough money to stop at Bierman's Ice Cream Parlor for a malt on the way home. After Katy was born, we didn't go much. Someone had to be with her all the time, and there was no money for a baby-sitter in addition to the cost of the movie. But now that Katy was nearly two, my mother had worked out an arrangement with another woman in our building. They took turns watching each other's babies; that way it didn't cost anything, and Mom said she worried less about Katy getting good care.

My father seldom went to the movies with us. He worked on the railroad and had to be gone at night much of the time. He had to go all the way to Fargo, stay there overnight, then return home the next day. Usually, he was home for two days and nights, but sometimes he was gone for several nights in a row. Mom called these long periods "doubling-out," which meant that Dad was making twice as many trips to Fargo as usual. She said he did this for us, so that there would be more money now that Katy was part of the family.

On most nights when my father was gone and there was no money to go to a movie or walk to Bierman's for ice cream, Mom read to Ron and me. We always sat on the couch that also served as my bed and brought stacks of our well-worn comic books to her. Sometimes Ron tried to sneak an extra one into his pile, which would start an argument. Mom ended these disagreements by counting out a limited but equal number for each of us. The three of us would finally settle onto the couch, Ron on mom's left side and me on her right.

Sometimes I tired of *Porky Pig* and *Little Lulu,* and asked to have poems read from Robert Louis Stevenson's book *A Child's Garden of Verses.* My favorite was about the lamplighter. I loved the part about growing up and lighting the streetlamps with him. It wasn't long before my mother knew all of the poems by heart, and I would sometimes watch her as she recited a poem without needing to look at the page.

When the evenings got particularly long, and neither Ron nor I got sleepy, she would tell us her throat was dry, and I would run and get a glass of water so that she would read just one more story or one more poem. It was always such a close, peaceful feeling, leaning against the softness and warmth of her arm and shoulder, and looking at pictures in the book as she read. I always wished she would go on reading forever.

But movies at the Franklin Theater generated pleasure of another, more exciting kind. On Wednesday night the three of us walked two blocks south to Franklin Avenue. Once we got to Franklin, it was just two short blocks east to the theater. We walked past Bierman's, where I wondered out loud if we might be able to stop for a malt on the way home. We walked past the Band Box Cafe, where we heard the jukebox playing and smelled the burgers and onions frying on the grill, and saw people laughing and drinking coffee from heavy white mugs that were rimmed with a green stripe. Just after we passed the Band Box, we arrived at the movie theater. The box office was bathed in an amber glow from the lobby lights and bulbs twinkled and rose like magical stars above the marquee. The air was heavy with the aroma of buttered popcorn. It wafted out the lobby doors, mingled with the crowd, then rose skyward with the blinking lights.

"We were lucky to be able to go tonight," my mother said. "They're giving away soup ladles. I've waited for one for over a year now."

"I'm glad, Mom," I said. I noticed that Ron hung his head and said nothing at all. It seemed to me that Ron was increasingly moody this summer, often silent and lost somewhere inside himself. "Lucky, isn't it, Ron?" I said and nudged my big brother.

"Yeah, real lucky," he said flatly.

The three of us waited in line, shuffling forward every few minutes. Dish-Night drew big crowds. I was glad that my mother was so excited about her soup ladle, but happier still that I was going to see *Robin Hood*, starring Errol Flynn. I had seen the movie once before but wanted to see it again. I didn't care much for the mushy parts, when Robin was kissing Maid Marian and telling her he loved her. The archery and sword fights and bringing Prince John to justice were what made the movie really worthwhile.

———

As we neared Bierman's on the way home, Mom said we could stop for a treat if Ron and I could agree on something to share.

"A malt! A chocolate malt!" I shouted. In my excitement I broke free of her hand and spun in front of Ron. I shouted my plea within inches of his face. "A malt! Come on, a chocolate malt!"

Ron stopped walking and glared at me. "Okay, stupid, a malt! Just shut up about it!" he shouted.

I was stunned motionless and silent. In an instant, the joy of the evening had vanished. Before I could do or say anything, Mom had jerked Ron by the arm so that he faced her.

"What is the matter with you?" she demanded.

"Nothing."

"That was a mean thing to say to your brother. Now you tell him you're sorry."

I watched as they faced each other. Ron's head was slightly bowed and I noticed for the first time that he was nearly as tall as Mom. She stared at him, her face taut with anger. "Tell him you're sorry," she repeated and gave his arm a shake.

"I'm sorry, Mike. I shouldn't have yelled at you," Ron mumbled.

"It's okay," I said quickly.

Mom's face softened again and she let go of Ron's arm. She put her hand under his chin and lifted his face. "You've been quiet and funny all night, Ron. Do you feel all right?"

Although Ron's face was almost level with hers, I could see in the light from Bierman's window that his eyes were cast down at the sidewalk. "Yeah, I'm fine, Mom."

"Are you sure?"

"Yeah, really. I'm just fine."

"All right then, let's enjoy ourselves. The three of us always have such good times together." She put her arms around both of us and gave us a hug. "Come on, let's go get that chocolate malt."

Despite the apology and my mother's attempts to be cheerful, Ron's sullenness persisted all the while we sat in Bierman's and drank our malt. I didn't understand what it was that had made him so silent and brooding, but I felt it really had nothing to do with my shouting about getting a malt. Even more upsetting was the feeling that my mother didn't understand Ron's mood any more than I did.

Just as we finished our malt, Mom picked up her new soup ladle and held it out for us to see. The handle was over a foot long, with a cup-shaped scoop at the end. It was made of metal covered with white enamel. There was a bright blue edging around the rim of the cup and along the handle. "Isn't this a great ladle?" she said.

"Sure is, Mom," I answered.

Ron looked down at the table and muttered something.

"I'm sorry, Ron, I couldn't hear you," Mom said.

Ron looked up at her. He had the same angry look as when he had shouted at me outside. "I said, if Dad didn't drink so much, you wouldn't have to get free dishes and crummy soup ladles!"

Mom sat back in her chair and dropped the ladle onto her lap. For an instant I thought she might cry. Her large brown eyes seemed to turn liquid and her mouth quivered almost imperceptibly. Then she glanced at me briefly. The message her eyes and mouth conveyed could not have been more eloquent if she had spoken aloud. My brother had said something I should not have heard. She stiffened in her chair. Now her eyes were clear, and there was a slight flush beneath the smooth, olive-tone skin of her cheeks. When she spoke, her words were firm and measured. "You have no right to criticize your father—none! How dare you speak against him!"

"It's true," Ron said.

Mom leaned forward, her eyes wide with anger. "Everything we have—everything—we owe to that man. No one loves his family more, or works harder to provide for them. And you dare to speak against him!"

"Yeah? Well, if he's so great, how come he drinks and yells at you?"

She raised her hand as if she might slap him. I turned my head away as I felt a sickening wave of tension deep in my stomach. When the sound of the slap didn't come, I looked back.

"You don't know your father. You don't know him at all. Yes, sometimes he drinks too much. And yes, sometimes he gets angry and loses his temper. Believe me, there are worse things. You have no right to judge him, and no real understanding of the responsibilities and problems he faces every day."

Ron spoke again, but with less conviction than before. "Other kids' dads don't drink like he does."

"I won't hear any more of this, young man. Not a word of it. Not one word. He's your father, and he loves you. He does the very best he can for all of us, and I won't sit here and listen to you speak against him. I don't ever"—she reached across the table and held Ron by the shoulders—"I don't ever want to hear you speak like that again. Do you understand me?"

"Yes."

"He's your father," she said with finality.

The three of us left Bierman's and walked home in silence. Dish-Night, *Robin Hood,* the treat at Bierman's were now cast in a strange, joyless shadow. Summer had just begun, a season of play and freedom and growing. But on this night, in the warm evening breeze, and somewhere inside each of us, were the first faint stirrings of a growing storm.

Three

On the day I introduced Ricky Stedman to two neighborhood kids, Harold and Keith, there was going to be a fight. Word had spread through our building that Swede and Tiny were going to settle an argument that had begun the previous night in Nile's Bar on Chicago Avenue. There were at least three different versions of why they were going to fight, but the true reason was of little or no concern. The only important fact was that they were going to meet at twelve-thirty in front of our building and settle their differences. By noon, the long stone steps that faced Elliot Avenue were already crowded with tenants awaiting what promised to be the most exciting event of the afternoon.

They crowded the steps, just as they sometimes did to watch someone move out of the neighborhood, or to read the paper and talk, or simply to sit on gray summer days, high up on the steps beneath the protection of the brick archway, and watch it rain. But, a fight was an unparalleled event that drew the largest, earliest gatherings. So, by the time my three friends and I arrived, there was no room left on the steps. We stood off to one side of the stone bleachers, back from the sidewalk where the gladiators were to meet.

One of the combatants, a large blond man called Swede, was already present. He stood before the crowd, staring north along Elliot Avenue, ignoring occasional shouts of "Get 'em, Swede!" and "You can take 'em!"

Ricky turned to me and said in a near-whisper, "I don't think my mom wants me here. She says fighting is evil, and we should see no evil."

I wanted him to stay with us, but found it difficult to argue with his mother's logic. "Well, maybe your dad won't care."

Ricky looked directly at me, his face devoid of emotion. "I don't have a dad," he said.

His statement struck me as so impossible that I didn't know how to respond. I hesitated for a moment, then decided to ignore what he had told me. "Just stay for a while," I pleaded.

"Yeah," Harold and Keith said in unison, "stick around, Ricky."

The crowd on the steps suddenly came to life. Shouts of encouragement to both participants filled the air. Some of the spectators stood to watch the man who advanced toward Swede along the avenue. He was a huge man, dressed in gray work pants and a matching shirt. The sleeves of his shirt were rolled up to the elbow, revealing muscular forearms thick with hair. He wore a wide black belt and black work boots. Other than his size, however, the most striking feature about him was his total baldness. His head looked like a mound of tanned flesh that bubbled up out of his neck. There weren't even eyebrows to help define his face.

Someone on the steps stood and shouted, "Kick his ass, Tiny!" The woman who sat next to this enthusiast slapped him on the arm and told him she would leave if he couldn't control himself. "Oh, come on, honey, don't spoil it," he said.

Ricky stood next to me, galvanized by the crowd's excitement. I knew he wouldn't leave now. Any thoughts of his mother's warning had obviously vanished.

The two men didn't speak, but slowly began to circle one another, fists raised to the level of their faces. The crowd was quiet now, and as the two men circled, I heard the one called Tiny speak. "I'm gonna hit ya, Swede," he growled. "I'm gonna knock ya into the next county."

Swede said nothing, but stumbled backward, as if Tiny's threat had carried with it an invisible force. Tiny pulled back his right arm, slowly, it seemed to me, then swung wildly in Swede's general direction. The punch missed its mark completely, but the force of the swing caused Tiny to lurch forward and nearly fall to the ground. He regained his balance, and the circling resumed.

The two men appeared to be engaged in some clumsy, hostile dance. They glared, they hurled insults and threats, they feinted and groaned and spat. They stopped, as if to take measure for the crushing blow, then began to circle again. The dance went on endlessly.

Impatient shouts went up from the crowd. Cries of "Get 'em!" and "Hit 'em, Tiny!" were mixed with laughter. The man who had been told earlier to control himself by the woman next to him now turned to her and said, "Hell, they're both drunk." This seemed to be understood by the crowd, but the common realization did nothing to dampen the collective enthusiasm. Shouts and laughter increased.

The two men appeared near collapse from their interminable dance. "I'm gonna kick ya, Tiny," Swede said. Swede stopped circling and began to move toward Tiny in a strange shuffle. With his right foot suspended several inches off the ground, he hopped forward on his left foot, all the time repeating, "I'm gonna kick ya, dammit!"

"Yeah, kick him, Swede," someone shouted from the steps, "but don't tell him first!"

The crowd roared with laughter, just as Swede made his final hop and kicked out with his right foot. For his effort, he completely lost his balance and crashed to the sidewalk on his back. Tiny now stood over the fallen man, taunting him while he made great circles in the air with his fists. "Get up, Swede! Come on, get up!"

People began to leave the steps, while those remaining shouted congratulations to Tiny. Swede, without question, had lost all heart and stomach for the fight. As the gathering thinned out, Tiny stood over his opponent, savoring his victory, rejoicing in Swede's decisive defeat. "Have you had enough, Swede?" he roared. "Have you had enough?" Swede glanced at his conqueror momentarily, then rolled onto his side for a nap.

Tiny raised his arms in victory. Scattered applause and laughter came from those who remained on the steps.

"That was a stupid fight," I said.

"Yeah," Ricky agreed, but I could see that he had not yet caught his breath. "Pretty big guys, though," he said.

Without my realizing it, my brother, Ron, had been watching the fight from behind us. "Mike's right," he said, "it was a stupid fight. If you guys really want to see something, why don't you come with me to Albinson's Mortuary."

Ricky looked at me. "What's that?" he said.

"It's where they keep dead people before they bury them," I said. "It's over on Chicago Avenue, at the other end of the block."

"Yeah, and I know a window where we can look in and see the bodies," Ron said.

"Not me," said Keith.

"Me neither," said Harold.

"Chickens," Ron said. "How about you, Ricky? How about you and Mike come with me?"

"I don't know, Ron," I said.

"Come on. I know where we can peek in and see the body before they fix it up for the funeral. The window is supposed to be all blacked out, but it isn't. If you crawl under the fence in the back and stay real low, you can see them get bodies ready for the funeral."

"Yuck," Harold said. "Who wants to see some dead body? I heard that sometimes they fart just as they're getting them ready."

"That's right," Keith joined in. "They fart and sometimes they even sit up. I heard that gas or something makes them sit right up like they're still alive."

Ricky turned from one speaker to the other. As each astonishing fact was stated, his eyes grew larger.

"Well," Ron said, "why don't you smart guys come with me and find out if all that's really true?"

Harold and Keith seemed to conspire with furtive glances.

"Sometimes they crap right on the table, too," Keith said. "Who wants to go watch some stiff fart and crap all over the place?"

"Yeah," Harold agreed.

"You two are just chicken," Ron said.

"We're not chicken," Keith said. "I've seen a dead person before. It's no big deal. I went to my uncle's funeral."

"It's not the same," Ron said. "It doesn't count."

"Does too," Keith said without much conviction.

Ron turned to Ricky and me, dismissing any chance of recruiting Keith or Harold for his expedition. "How about it, Mike? How about you and Ricky coming with me?"

I turned to look at Ricky. His face was pale and his blue eyes seemed ready to explode out of their sockets. "I gotta get home," he said. "I gotta go right now." With that, he ran across the street, not even bothering to watch for cars or to look back.

"Bunch of chickens," Ron said. "Maybe I'll just have to go alone." He turned and began to walk away from us, with a certain heroic bearing in the way he squared his shoulders.

"Sometimes they say things when they sit up, too!" Keith shouted after him. "Sometimes they say the word they said most often in their life. It's really stupid!"

———

That night, just before we went to bed, Ron told me he had gone alone to the mortuary. He had slipped under the fence and crawled to one of the basement windows. But the window was painted black and he couldn't see anything. He said he figured that someone who worked there must have realized kids had found a way to look in and had painted the window over again. I was glad he hadn't seen anything. It seemed wrong to me somehow that anybody, unless they had to, should look at a dead person as they got them ready for their funeral. It just seemed to me that you should be left alone at that time, especially if you made a mess of yourself.

I told my mother about Ricky Stedman saying he had no father. I told her I knew that was impossible, but I hadn't said anything. She told me I was right not to question him and that it was possible that Ricky's mother and father were divorced. She said that him saying he had no father only meant that for some reason his father was no longer part of their family. She said it would be impolite for me to ask about it, and if Ricky wanted me to know any more, he would tell me.

Four

Katy's birthday came in July. She would be two, and I wanted to do something special for her. I didn't have money for a present, but I thought it would be a great gift if I could take her for a ride around the block in our Radio Flyer wagon. I could show her Leo's Ice House, Rotograph's, the bakery, Albinson's Mortuary, and all the houses along Elliot Avenue. She could see the street-cars, too, as they clattered along Chicago Avenue. I knew she loved them; she would always squeal and point and clap her hands whenever she saw one.

With Mom's help, I prepared the wagon for Katy's ride. We dropped the cross-work of red wooden rails into the metal brackets on the side of the wagon so that Katy could sit up and I wouldn't have to worry about her falling out. We lined the bottom of the wagon with a pillow and blanket for a comfortable ride. I promised I would keep a close eye on Katy and not go anywhere other than around the block. I was not to cross any streets, run, or try to do any tricks with the wagon. After all this preparation and instruction, I kissed my mother good-bye and began Katy's birthday ride.

We had only gone as far as the ice house when we were stopped. Leo made me bring the wagon over to where he was sitting. I think it was the first time I ever saw Leo stand up and leave his chair. He walked the few steps to the wagon and looked down at Katy. "Well, well, what do we have here?" he said and chuckled.

"This is my sister, Katy," I said with inordinate pride. "It's her birthday today, and I'm taking her for a ride around the block."

Leo exhaled a gentle "Oh." He leaned forward to get a closer look. "Her birthday! A special day, isn't it?" he whispered.

Katy looked up at the stranger and smiled. She looked beautiful to me. She had on her only dress—pink with white lace around the shoulders and neck. Her hair, a light brown, appeared to pale in the sunlight. It surrounded her generous, smooth cheeks and large, glistening eyes, framing them in a shifting, golden border.

"And do you know how old you are today?" Leo asked.

Katy held up two fingers, V-shaped.

"Two years old!" Leo exclaimed.

Katy nodded.

"My, my—that's a great age to be," Leo chuckled. "That's a perfect age."

Katy nodded agreement.

"And such a pretty girl! You're very pretty, Katy Dougherty. Did you know that?"

"Yes," Katy said with equanimity.

Leo threw back his head and roared so loud with laughter it seemed to frighten Katy. "Oh my," Leo said as he recovered, "she has her mother's French good looks and her father's Irish wit."

I wasn't sure what Leo meant, but it bothered me that he

evidently knew so much about our family. Talking with Leo always ended up an uncomfortable matter at best. "We have to go now," I said. "I can't keep Katy out too long or my mom will get worried."

"Now just a minute," Leo said. "Just hold on, I think I've got something for your sister here." Leo shoved his hand deep into a pocket of his trousers. "I want you to buy a treat for your little sister on her birthday."

After some searching, Leo extracted a tarnished coin from his pocket and held it out to Katy. "I'm giving this nickel to your brother. You have him buy a Popsicle for the two of you. You like Popsicles?"

Katy nodded.

"Well, you have your brother buy one for you. That's your present from old Leo."

"Thank you," Katy said.

"You're very welcome, honey."

I took the nickel from Leo and promised to buy a Popsicle for Katy and me. I thanked Leo again for both of us and resumed our tour of the block. Before I had even gotten the wagon back on the sidewalk, Leo shouted, "That would be a great wagon for hauling ice! You and your brother could haul fifty-pound blocks of ice in a wagon like that." I just waved without looking back.

———

Katy's trip was a great success. I took her out of the wagon and into Rotograph's for our Popsicle. I showed her the fountain that held every imaginable flavor, and helped her count the handles that released the rainbows of syrup. We saw Nile's Bar, which I explained to Katy was a place we weren't allowed to enter, but in any event, I was sure, wasn't nearly as nice as Rotograph's. She saw Albinson's Mortuary, but I didn't tell her about the dead people inside. Twice along Chicago Avenue we saw a streetcar, and Katy applauded both of them with unrestrained delight. Even the sky looked scrubbed and bright for her day, like the sky on an old postcard my mother had saved. She had shown the card to me at least a dozen times, and talked about having it framed. She had told me it was a picture of a painting by a famous French artist named Claude Monet. It was right, I thought, that Katy should have a sky by Monet—water-blue with towering, expansive clouds that stood still and silent above the earth.

———

We were having a special meal that night. Mom had baked a birthday cake with white frosting, two candles, and "Happy Birthday Katy" spelled out in an unbroken swirl of green icing. The dinner was Katy's favorite, spaghetti with meatballs. The table was set for all five of us, with the cake as the centerpiece. Mom timed the meal to be ready at seven, when my father was due home from work.

Ron and I sat with Katy on the couch and looked at comic books while we waited for our father. Her favorite was *Little Lulu,* and she enjoyed looking at the pictures even if her interest in the story was difficult to sustain. After five or six comics, Ron began to ask Mom at regular intervals about the time, and why she thought Dad wasn't home. When it was nearly eight, we had lost all interest in comics and wanted only to eat the meal that was being shifted back and forth on the stove and kept warm. We were each allowed one piece of buttered bread with sugar, which we were told would keep us from getting painfully hungry, but would not ruin our appetites for dinner.

About eight-thirty Mom made a phone call and found out that my father's train had arrived on time. After she made the call, she began to pick at her fingernails, first one hand, then the other. She said we would wait a little longer before we ate. She didn't say any more, but periodically walked to the front window, digging nervously at her nails. I could hear the clicking of nail against nail each time she walked past me on her way to the window.

Katy had fallen asleep on the couch by the time my father arrived. Even the slamming of the door and the heavy thud of his suitcase on the floor failed to wake her. He stood just inside the doorway, a tall, muscular man in a dark blue brakeman's uniform. He stayed near the entrance—a massive, brooding figure who stood not quite in darkness, and not quite in light.

He took off his uniform hat and dropped it on top of his suitcase. "Jean!" he shouted without moving. "Jean! What the hell are these kids still doing up at this hour?"

Mom went to him and stood close, as if she were examining him. Ron and I stayed on the couch, next to the sleeping Katy.

"We were waiting for you," she said. "We've been waiting to celebrate Katy's birthday. I baked a cake for her. I thought we'd all have dinner together."

My father said nothing. He walked to the dinner table and looked at the empty plates and the untouched birthday cake. He appeared to stumble slightly to one side, just a fleeting, almost imperceptible moment of imbalance. "Happy Birthday Katy," he read out loud.

"Pat, did you forget?" Mom said. She spoke the words softly, without anger or accusation, but with a sort of quiet melancholy.

My father turned to face her. He leaned back against the

table. "No, I didn't forget. Don't start accusing me of forgetting my children's birthdays!"

"I wasn't accusing—"

"You didn't say one goddamn word about having a party for her tonight, did you?" My father's voice was pressured and full of anger.

"No."

"No! But you're all set to raise hell with me because I'm a little late for a birthday party you never told me about."

"I'm sorry, Pat. I just thought—"

"You just thought," he spat out the words. "You thought what? What the hell did you think?" he shouted.

Mom looked small and frightened as she backed away from him. "Please, Pat," she said, "not in front of the boys."

"What?" he shouted as he pushed away from the table and moved toward her.

"Please, Pat. I know you've been drinking and I don't want to fight with you."

"There it is," my father roared. "That's it! I've been drinking, that's the whole problem. That's the whole goddamn thing. I can't stop with my friends and have one goddamn drink after work."

"Please, Pat—"

"You know what I feel like doing? You know what I should do? I ought to walk out that goddamn door and get drunk. I come home to this kind of bullshit, and I just want to walk right back out that door and really get drunk!"

"I'm sorry, Pat," my mother said.

"Sorry? You're sorry? No, *I'm* sorry. I'm sorry I have to come home to this kind of crap after being on the road all night and all day. It's no goddamn wonder I need a few drinks before I come home." He turned and slammed his fist on the table, hard enough to rattle the plates. "For two goddamn cents, I'd walk out that door right now!" he shouted.

Katy awakened to the sound of my father's rage and began to cry. "Quiet, Katy," I said, and tried to shield her from the sight of my parents by hugging her to my chest.

"Now you've got the goddamn kid crying!" my father raged. He walked into the tiny kitchen and began pulling covers off pots on the stove. He tossed the covers carelessly to the floor. He took one of the pots and walked back to the table. "Here! Here, come and eat your spaghetti. Let's all have some goddamn spaghetti and get to bed."

"Stop it!" my mother said and grabbed at his arm.

"Here!" my father bellowed and threw a cold wad of noodles at one of the plates. "Here!" he shouted again, and pitched a second handful of spaghetti at the table. "Here!" he shouted and threw a third wad that landed on the cake.

"Stop it!" my mother screamed and pulled at his arm.

"Get the hell out of my way. Get the hell out of my way! Right now!"

Mom stepped aside just as Ron bolted from the couch and ran toward my father. She caught Ron around the waist and held him tight. "I hate you!" Ron screamed at my father as he struggled to free himself from Mom's grasp. "You're drunk and I hate you!"

Mom held on tight and whispered desperately to him. "Stop, Ron. Don't say that to your father. Don't ever say things like that to your father," she repeated as the tears welled up in her eyes and ran down her cheeks.

As quickly as my father's rage had erupted, it subsided. In only a matter of minutes, he left the table and without a word went to the bedroom. In his wake, my mother comforted us and did her best to brush away the tears and anger and fear. Each of us was given a reheated portion of the remaining spaghetti, which I choked down only out of a sense of duty. We all had a small piece of cake, after noodles were carefully removed from the frosting. We didn't sing to Katy, and there were no presents to open. My mother, with gentle, soothing tones and light, loving strokes of our heads and backs, tried her utmost to bring some element of normality to what was left of the evening.

Later, when my bed was made and I settled onto the couch for the night, I tried not to think of my father. I knew that in the morning everything would be changed. He would be tired, perhaps sick, and full of remorse for what he had done. I had witnessed this sort of upheaval before, and prayed each time that I would never see it again. I turned on my side, wrapping myself in my comforter, my back to the dining room and the ugliness of what had happened.

Five

For reasons I didn't immediately understand, Ron was planning an assault on Nile's Bar. He had worked out in elaborate detail an attack that was to take place on a Thursday night. His plan, he assured me, was flawless. However, it could only be executed with Ricky's and my help. Our recruitment, it turned out, was the most difficult step in the campaign. But, through Ron's persuasion and persistence, we became his reluctant lieutenants.

On Thursday nights, when my father was on the road, Mom visited one of the other women in our building. Ron and I were left alone with Katy for an hour or so during these visits. It was at this time, after Katy was asleep, that Ron had determined we could sneak out of the apartment and launch our attack on the bar.

In the laundry room of our building, just behind the back door of our apartment, a cardboard box filled with water balloons awaited us beneath one of the laundry tubs. Ron and Ricky and I had spent over an hour earlier in the day filling penny balloons with water. The balloons had been tied off and carefully placed in the box, then hidden for later retrieval.

After Katy was asleep and our box of balloons plucked from the laundry room, we left to get Ricky.

"Don't drop any of those balloons," Ron rasped as we scurried across the street.

"I won't," I said. I tightened my hold on the box as I felt the liquid cargo shift from side to side.

"Ricky better be ready."

"He will be," I said.

We ran up the embankment and around the side of the house to Ricky's bedroom window. Ron scratched at the screen on the window with his fingernail. Two short scratches was the signal. As we waited for Ricky to appear, I noted the light of the moon to be more brilliant and piercing than I had ever seen it. The light was haunting and sinister. It illuminated everything, casting shadows of blue on blue, exposing houses and fences and garbage cans and young boys of felonious intent. It gave Ricky's face a pale, bloodless quality when he appeared at the window.

"Unlock the screen," Ron whispered. "Come on, we haven't got much time."

Ricky hesitated. "I don't know . . . ," he said.

"Come on. We won't get caught, and it's a bad place, Ricky. Rotten people go there."

Ricky released the hook at the base of the screen and pushed against the wooden frame. Ron held the screen out away from the house until Ricky had clambered out and landed with a thud on the ground.

A key element of Ron's plan was a wooden fence located behind the businesses facing Chicago Avenue. It ran parallel to the alley for nearly half a block. The fence was over six feet high. Ron theorized that none of the bar patrons could scale the fence, yet we were all small enough to scamper under it at a point behind

Nile's Bar. He had deepened a depression in the ground in preparation for this night, and had even practiced crawling back and forth under the fence at this critical spot. He assured us that we would all fit easily, while no full-grown adult could possibly take advantage of our route. Anyone in pursuit would have no choice but to run around the fence, allowing us ample time to make our escape.

The water balloons were to be dropped through a skylight located directly above the bar. Ron had already climbed the old wooden steps at the back of the building and surveyed the roof and skylight. One side of the skylight could be pried open wide enough for two boys to pitch a barrage of water balloons in a matter of seconds. By the time the people in the bar realized what had happened, the marauders would already have vanished.

The three of us crossed Elliot Avenue and headed west toward the alley and our target.

"We'll have to circle around the fence," Ron said. "The box won't fit under it."

Ricky and I both nodded.

"Wait a second," Ron said and called our advance to a halt. "Ricky's going to be the lookout. He'll have to stand at the back of the building and watch for anyone who might be coming toward the alley between Nile's and the bakery. We're going to need a signal. Can you whistle real loud?"

"No," Ricky said, "I can't whistle at all."

"Damn," Ron said, but he was frustrated for only a moment. He reached out and held Ricky by the shoulders. "Can you make a real high sound like this? *Eeek! Eeek!*" Ron demonstrated a shrill, throaty squeal.

"I think so."

"Try it," Ron said.

"Eeek! Eeek!" The sound was even higher and more piercing than Ron's.

"Perfect!" Ron said, and clapped him on the shoulders. "Me and Mike will take the box up to the roof. You stay down on the ground and watch for anyone between the bar and the bakery. If you see anybody, you give the signal. Okay?"

"Eeek! Eeek!" Ricky replied.

"Great. Just great," Ron said. "One other thing. If we get chased by anyone, we split up."

"I thought you told me nobody could chase us?" I said.

"This is just in case, Mike. I don't think anybody can get us. But even if someone does run after us, if we split up they won't know which way to run. Then, later, we'll meet back at Ricky's house. Okay?"

"Okay," I said.

Ricky was busy practicing a subdued version of his signal.

"Did you hear what I said?" Ron asked.

"Yeah, we meet back at my house."

"Okay," Ron said, "let's go."

The three of us crossed the alley and followed the fence south until it ended near Rotograph's. We slipped around the end of the fence and headed north for the back of Nile's Bar and our target. We hurried along, needlessly bent from the waist in a posture of stealth, shushing each other when one of us accidentally kicked a can or bottle. By the time we reached the wooden steps that rose to within climbing distance of the roof of the bar, I could feel my heart pounding wildly in my chest. The thumping, which I was sure had to be audible, was not from exertion but an unprecedented sense of fear and adventure.

"This is it," Ron said. "Ricky, you stay right here. You watch between the buildings. If you see anybody, you give the signal. Okay?"

"Okay."

Ron turned to me. "I'll go up first. When I get on the roof, you hand me the box, then I'll help you up."

Ron and I started up the steps, leaving our sentry to stand his lonely watch. Ron and I shushed each other as the steps creaked beneath our feet. When we reached the top, we stood on a landing that faced a locked screen door. A wooden railing that bordered the landing provided our access to the roof. Ron climbed on top of the railing, and with practiced skill pulled himself up onto the roof.

"Okay, Mike, get on the railing and hand the box up to me."

"I can't," I said. "It's impossible."

"It isn't impossible at all. Just set the box on the railing, then you get on the railing and hand it up. Don't turn chicken on me now!"

For the moment, my anger with Ron surpassed all other emotions. "I won't do it, Ron. What if I fall? I could die!"

"You won't fall, and you won't die, stupid!"

The debate didn't last long. Ron's unique combination of insults, encouragement, and threats eventuated in my tumbling onto the roof beside him.

"See, I told you it wasn't impossible. I told you you wouldn't die."

"Yeah," I said, "but I might die on the way back down."

Ron shook his head. "Going down is easier. We just hang from the edge of the roof and drop onto the landing. Come on now, time's running out."

We crept to the skylight, as my heart thundered out its renewed signal of alarm. Now my legs betrayed me, too. They felt weak and uncontrollable. They shook and gave way as Ron pried open the skylight.

"Give me two balloons," Ron said.

I handed him the balloons and then took two for myself. We leaned over the open skylight and peered down on the bar and its patrons.

There were a dozen or more men at the dimly lit bar. Most of them sat on stools. Some stood facing the bar, and one teetered and swayed alone in front of the jukebox. Their voices blended into a low, ominous droning sound, like beasts engaged in some horrible, secret ritual.

"When I say 'fire,' we let 'em go. Then grab some more and pitch 'em in."

"Okay."

"Ready . . . aim . . . fire!"

I saw my first balloon hit the bar and bounce, intact, onto the floor. The second hit the floor directly and exploded into a dark, pear-shaped puddle. One of Ron's balloons struck a glass, causing it to tip and spin along the bar, spraying beer and water on two men. I lost track of the fourth bomb. Neither Ron nor I continued to watch, but frantically grabbed balloons and pitched them into the bar with abandon.

We could hear men shouting from below. Cries of "What the hell!" and "God damn it!" and "Jesus Christ!" burst up through the skylight and into the clear night air.

"Run for it, Mike!" Ron shouted as he sprinted toward the back of the building.

I ran after him, lost my balance, and sprawled face-first onto the roof's graveled surface. As I picked myself up, palms scraped raw from the gravel, I heard an ear-piercing shriek of *"Eeek! Eeek!"*

"Hurry, Mike!" Ron shouted as he hung from the edge of the roof. "Hurry up! I'll drop down on the landing and catch you."

When I reached the edge of the building, Ron was already on the landing, coaching me to hang and drop to the sound of his voice. "Come on, let go! I'll catch you. Hurry up, someone's coming!"

A voice broke out of the darkness, sending a wave of fear that pried my fingers loose from the brick. I fell, longer and further than I imagined. I tumbled through the dark space, suspended for a moment without foundation or support or contact of any kind. I crashed onto the wooden landing, my brother's arms around my chest, holding me up. "Run, Mike!" he said, as soon as I regained my balance.

"What the hell is going on out here?" The words boomed out of the darkness. This time, I recognized the voice. It was Tiny! The pugnacious Tiny. Tiny of the great fight. Tiny of the black boots and the hairy arms.

As we reached the bottom of the steps, I saw Ricky scramble under the fence. Tiny was just off to the right of the steps, his back to us. He had evidently seen Ricky and chased him to our secret escape route.

"Run for it!" Ron shouted.

On hearing Ron's command, Tiny turned in our direction. "Come here, you little shit!" he roared as he reached out for me.

I ducked beneath his huge hand and bellied my way under the fence. When I got to the other side, I stopped to look back and see Ron emerge from the hole, safely out of Tiny's grasp.

"Run!" Ron shouted as Tiny's dark image loomed above the fence. Suddenly, Tiny was on the ground and running toward me.

"Come here, you little bastard! Don't make me chase you!"

I could hear the thud of his boots and feel my lungs struggling for air as I ran. The boots drew closer, their rhythm broken only by Tiny's vile threats. The distance between us was closing, and I knew my only chance was to hide.

I ran around the corner of the building, stopped and squatted down next to a trash can. I made myself as small as I could. I hugged my legs against my body and peeked out above my knees. The wall of the building hid me from the light of the traitorous moon. I tried to will my heart to silence and my breathing to a deadly stillness.

The boots came closer, then slowed to a walk. I looked only at the ground, afraid that if I looked up I would be seen. I watched the boots walk past me, and heard them fade and finally stop.

"Where'd the little shit go?" Tiny asked himself.

I held my position and waited. The boots approached again, stopped, then headed back toward the alley and Nile's Bar. For the first time, I became aware of the pungent odor of the garbage and the raw stinging of my palms. But, I waited in silence until I was convinced that Tiny had given up the search completely.

I left my hiding place and ran to Ricky's house. When I arrived at Ricky's bedroom window there was no one in sight.

"Psst!" came from behind a bush. "Mike?"

"Yeah."

"Did you get caught?"

"No," I said to the bush.

Ron and Ricky appeared from the foliage. "We did it," Ron said. "We got them, and nobody got caught."

Ricky smiled and said nothing.

"I almost got caught," I said, "and I hurt my hands when I fell on the roof."

Ron put his arm across my back. "You're okay, Mike. We'll get Ricky back in his house, then go home and I'll help you clean up." He squeezed my shoulder in a one-armed hug. "We got them good!" he said.

Our entire adventure had taken less than an hour. Katy had slept through our great raid on Nile's Bar, peacefully unaware of the heroics and daring deeds of her brothers. Someday, when she was older, I thought, we could tell her about the night in great detail. I knew she would appreciate our skill and bravery, experiencing vicariously an assault worthy of Robin Hood himself.

Six

More and more that summer, I came to think of my father as two people. When he drank too much, which seemed to occur with increasing frequency, he was unpredictable and explosive and often cruel. The smallest matter could cause an outburst of rage and violence. A light left on in a room, the slightest disagreement between Ron and me, Katy crying because she had fallen, the subtlest, most unfortunate choice of words by Mom—any of these could trigger a storm of hostility. Looking back, I believe that even at such an early age I began to see that his rage, somehow, was not really related to these tiny frustrations of life. With a child's logic, I vaguely understood that his demons did not exist in the external world, but dwelt somewhere within him. If there was no cause for anger, one could be invented, so that when he drank, nothing could ensure tranquillity. The blinding flash of his temper could be ignited by anything—or by nothing at all.

When he wasn't drinking—periods that lasted as long as a month at times—he kept his troubles to himself. Never a man to show much physical affection toward us, he expressed whatever feelings of tenderness he had in the most oblique way. Gestures of love were inarticulate and rare, leaving us to guess at their meaning. Ron quickly tired of this speculation and distanced himself from Dad. Increasingly, Ron greeted the most overt offers of closeness with indifference and stony silence. In contrast, my persistent, unspoken hope was that Dad's drinking was a temporary aberration that would fade and finally vanish, and I hungered to respond to those fleeting moments of kindness. I knew that this was the man my mom loved, the man she defended and understood and forgave. I believed, too, my mom knew that someday Dad's drinking would be a thing of the past.

One of those treasured opportunities for closeness came unexpectedly as I watched my father shaving on a Wednesday morning. I stood in the doorway of the bathroom, fascinated by the process. I watched closely as he swirled a brush in his cream-colored shaving cup, then dabbed at his face with the brush until he wore a full beard of foamy white. Before he began to shave, he turned and looked down at me, a hint of a smile creasing the white beard. "Would you like to go to Fargo with me on Friday?"

"Yeah!" I said. Memories of a trip Ron and I had taken with Dad the previous winter surfaced in my thoughts. We had gone with him on the train from St. Paul to Fargo, a stretch of land that was half the world to a boy of eight. He had worked through the night, passing swiftly through towns that were only patches of orange light in the vast fields of Minnesota snow. Elk River, Wadena, Hawley, Dilworth—names of places that existed only as temporary stops on a ceaseless journey.

The trip had given me a vague sense of wisdom from what I considered a privileged view of life. Ron and I had struggled to stay awake through the night, trying to remember the name of the next town, and the next, until we reached Fargo. I had thought of my friends sleeping in familiar beds, as we moved northward on our single-minded mission. I had stood at the rear of the last coach and watched the lights of the city until they were no more than a silver glow against the dark winter sky, and my little world and its problems had become distant and insignificant.

"Is Ron going, too?" I asked.

Dad watched himself in the mirror as he shaved. "I can only take one of you this time," he said without looking at me.

While part of me was disappointed, at the same time it made the trip more special. "Okay," I said, seizing the chance to be with him.

On Friday evening I stood beside my father in the busy waiting room of the Union Depot in St. Paul. I tried to be patient while he finished a conversation with an obese man who appeared to have a cigar permanently attached to one corner of his mouth. I watched the unlit cigar with some small interest, not listening to the conversation until I heard my name mentioned.

"This is my son Mike," Dad said to the man with the cigar.

"You gonna be a railroad man like your daddy?" he said, looking down at me only with his eyes, the head continuing to face my father.

"I don't know," I said.

"I think he'll do better than that, Art," Dad said, to my disappointment. "He's a pretty smart boy."

"Well, have a good trip," Art said and raised a huge hand to his waist in a sort of half-wave. "Nice to have met you, son."

"Nice to meet you, sir," I said.

We hurried through the waiting room toward the concourse and the numbered gates. When we reached the gate where our train was waiting, I felt the excitement rise in me as we walked down the concrete steps to the platform. As we passed through the double doors and out onto the platform, clouds of steam hissed from beneath the train and swept across the walkway, momentarily hiding our path. My senses were overwhelmed with the sight and sound of the trains, and the romantic, unique odor of steam and burning coal and axle grease.

"Stick close to me," Dad said. "Don't get in the way of those baggage carts."

I hurried to keep up with him, my legs working at a fast march. Scowling drivers noisily maneuvered carts with baggage and mail up and down the concourse with abandon, and the steam continued to burst periodically from beneath the coaches, like a funhouse at a great fair.

"We'll go in here," he said, motioning me toward one of the coaches.

We sat in a corner seat, where my father reversed one of the seatbacks and created a compartment large enough for four people. He placed his lantern and suitcase on the seat across from us. I took the corner by the window, leaving the aisle seat for my father.

"We'll be taking on passengers now. Don't let anyone sit here. I'll be back in a little while," he said as he pulled on his gloves and headed back outside with his lantern.

Through the window, I saw him on the platform with the yellow metal stool that served as a first step for the passengers. He looked proud and strong in his fresh blue uniform, a handsome man with jet-black hair and eyes of crystalline blue. I watched him direct people to the proper coaches, and I could imagine nothing finer than to be a railroad man like my father and his father before him. I wondered why he told people he doubted that I would work on the road. I wondered if he felt there was something lacking in me, some strength or ability which had simply failed to take.

Passengers filed clumsily through the coach, bumping suitcases against the seats and making abortive attempts to fling them atop the overhead rack. I kept a stern face, as a silent warning to them not to sit in the seats reserved for my father and me.

In a short time Dad was beside me as the train began to move slowly out of the station. I watched the rails next to us, silver paths that separated, converged, then ran off in different directions. I watched them until we were out of the station, beyond the cover of the train sheds.

"Well, we're on our way," my father said.

"Dad, why do you always tell people I probably won't work on the road? Your father worked on the road, didn't he?"

"Yes, he did. So did my brother, and my uncle, and all the Doughertys I can remember," he said, not answering my real question.

I persisted. "Why don't you want me to work on the railroad?"

He didn't look at me, but opened his suitcase and searched for the thermos of coffee my mother had made earlier that evening. He closed the suitcase and used it as a table for two metal cups. "Would you like some coffee?" he said.

"Just a little bit," I said. I took only a quarter of a cup, as a concession to the fact that I was not allowed to drink it at home and knew Mom didn't want me drinking it under any circumstances. I waited to ask my question again.

"There's no future in railroading," Dad said, anticipating me.

I wasn't sure what he meant, so I didn't say anything more about it. "Is there only one stop tonight?"

"That's right. We'll stop at Staples, then it's straight through to Fargo."

"What time do you think we'll get to Fargo?"

"We should get in about one in the morning," he said and checked his gold pocket watch as he spoke. "Mom packed a lunch for us. Are you hungry?"

"I don't know," I said. "Are you?"

He smiled almost imperceptibly. "I usually wait until we reach the division point at Staples before I eat."

"What time do we get there?"

"About ten. It's a long wait. Go ahead and have a sandwich if you're hungry."

"No," I said. "I think I'll wait until the division point."

I sipped a little coffee and slid back deep into the seat, comfortable with the rhythmic movement of the coach. I waited to see the first town on our trip—Elk River. After Elk River came St. Cloud then Little Falls and Cushing and Lincoln, and finally the division point at Staples.

—

A little before ten I walked to the last vestibule and watched the tracks dissolve into the night as I listened to the constant drum of the wheels. I stood in the cool evening wind and felt the coach rumble and sway beneath my feet. I held on to the cold steel of the handrail, squeezing it as tightly as I could. I wanted the moment to be as strong and real as I could make it, so that the memory would be as ageless as the metal in my hand.

"Why don't you come and sit down?" Dad said, breaking through my thoughts. "We'll be in Staples in a few minutes, we've just got time for a little coffee."

By the time we reached Staples, I was growing sleepy in the warmth and quiet of the dimly lit coach and the stillness of the halted train. I decided to step outside and see my father. He had said the stop would only last a little more than ten or fifteen minutes, and I thought a brief time in the night air might revive me.

Dad was talking with someone when I got outside. He was an older man, with a broad-brimmed hat pulled down so tightly that it touched the back of his shirt. Both his hands were shoved deep into the pockets of his pants, and I could see a pinpoint of red light from a cigarette that dangled from his lips. He and my father spoke in quiet tones, and I sensed there was something wrong about the situation.

I walked to them and stood beside my father. Neither man acknowledged my presence. I listened, unable to understand the mumblings of the man in the hat. My father told the man he should go home and sleep.

I stayed near the train and watched the two of them walk slowly toward the depot's waiting room, my father half-guiding, half-pushing the man along. They went inside and I could see that my father was doing all the talking now. I saw my father reach into his pocket and then press something into the man's hand. They seemed to argue a bit, then the man shook my father's hand and left the depot. I watched the stranger shuffle along, swaying from side to side as he headed toward the town.

My father ran back to the train, shouting for me to go inside and take my seat. He seemed upset, almost angry.

For a time we sat without speaking and silently shared the lunch my mother had packed. Finally, I asked about the stranger.

The man's name was Bill Tracy, and he was a retired brakeman. He was a young man when, in June of 1915, my father's uncle Al had died in a wreck near Hazelton. There had been a heavy rain and the engine had overturned on a stretch of softened roadbed. Only Al and the fireman were killed. Bill Tracy had been on the train.

Dad's voice seemed thick and strained. I looked closely at him. He appeared suddenly older, with tiny lines near the corners of his pale eyes. "I'm afraid Bill had way too much to drink tonight. When he gets like that, he comes down to the depot and bothers people with stories about when he was young. When they don't pretend to listen to him anymore, he goes back to some dreary little place he has in town."

I had heard my father tell about the death of his uncle before, but I had never heard of Bill Tracy. "Was he a good friend of your uncle?" I asked.

"I don't know. I was just about your age when Uncle Al died. And I remember Bill coming to the funeral, but I don't know if they were very close. He claims they were good friends, but it happened so long ago, I don't think he really knows the truth anymore."

I looked out the window. The lights of Staples were no longer visible, only the gray and black countryside of the August night. I tried to forget about Bill Tracy, and about my father's reaction to him. I finished my sandwich and tried to remember the next town on the way to Fargo. Wadena. After Wadena came New York Mills, then Frazee, then Detroit Lakes.

"He seemed very sad," I said without thinking.

"Yes, he is very sad," Dad said. He looked at me as though my words had carried some great truth. "He has nothing, only memories that are confused and meaningless to everyone but him. He never really gave himself to anything, or anyone, and now he's living out the result of that."

"What do you mean?"

My father let out a long, relief-giving sigh and stretched his legs so that they rested on the seat opposite us. "Nothing. Just that he was a very hopeful man once, and now he is a very sad and lonely man, with no one to care for him. He never understood what he really wanted."

"Do you like him?" I asked.

My father smiled at me. "I suppose so," he said. He smiled again, then gathered up the sandwich wrappings and the thermos and put them in his suitcase.

"Would you like to walk up to the head end and see the conductor with me?"

"No, I think I'll stay here," I said, glad that he was smiling again.

"All right. Maybe you should get a little sleep, you look awfully tired."

"I want to stay awake until Fargo," I said with a yawn.

"It isn't important, you know."

"I know," I said. "It's just something I'd like to do."

"Okay. Just relax and enjoy the ride. Don't let the thing with Bill Tracy upset you."

"I won't."

I lay across the seat and rested my head on a pillow created from my father's uniform coat. I tried to figure out what he meant when he said that Bill Tracy had never understood what he really wanted. Perhaps Dad was angry because Bill drank too much or because he had no family or because he may have lied about being Al's good friend. I couldn't understand it, so I thought about other, more pleasant things.

I thought of reaching Fargo in the warm, silent night. I thought of my father and walking with him the few short blocks to the hotel, where we would sleep late into the morning. I thought of how lucky I was to have this time with him and how much I hoped he would never drink again. If he could stay as he was on this night, then nothing could ever spoil the things we did together—not strange, lonely men, or anything else in the world.

Seven

As summer progressed, Ricky and I were together constantly. On rainy days and sometimes in the evening, when we couldn't play outside, we would be at my apartment listening to the radio or reading comics. There was *Gang Busters* and *The Shadow* and *The Green Hornet* and *Straight Arrow* and *The Lone Ranger* on the radio. For evening shows, my mother would turn off the lights in the living room and we would gather in front of the illuminated dial of the old wooden Philco and imagine the sights of speeding cars and galloping horses and arrows shot straight and true. Occasionally she would make fudge for us, and we would clean the plate as we listened to the demise of western outlaws and modern gangsters.

On Saturdays, when Dad was on the road, Mom would walk four blocks north with all of us to Elliot Park. She said she always enjoyed the walk, and that the fresh air was good for Katy. Mom said she enjoyed having Ricky with us, too, because he was so well mannered and quiet. She would sit on one of the park benches, gently rolling Katy's stroller back and forth while Ron and Ricky and I waded in the public pool. She told me she had no difficulty knowing where we were at any time. She only needed to look in the direction of the pool and Ricky's blazing carrot-colored hair would snare her eye.

At times, when Katy was restless, my mother would leave her bench and push the stroller around the park. The curbed side-walks led past the pool and the swings and picnic tables where old men spent countless hours playing checkers and feeding pigeons. The old men, bent with age, some bearded, would leave the pigeons and stop their games to smile and talk to Katy. They would tip their hats to my mother and tell her what a beautiful child she had. After they fussed and smiled and made an assortment of comic faces at Katy, they would back away with a kind of public-park reverence. My mother graciously accepted this homage to herself and her daughter, smiling and thanking the old men for their compliments. She would walk on after these flattering delays, carrying herself proudly.

It didn't occur to me that we never spent any time at Ricky's house and seldom saw his mother. I had nearly forgotten about the day we met Ricky, and how his mother had been so anxious to remove him from our company. I had also come to accept his curious remark about having no father as the natural order of things, even if it was unexplored and not fully understood. My relative ignorance of Ricky's family and home might have gone on indefinitely, had I not told him about my train trip to Fargo with my father. We sat in the warmth of the early morning sun on the bottom step in front of my building, as Ricky listened intently to the story of my train trip. I told him I would ask my father if he could go with us sometime.

"Would you?!" Ricky said.

"Yeah, I will. It might be a long time, though." I thought for a moment. "Maybe a year."

Ricky hung his head and began to dig with a stick at a crack in the sidewalk. "I went on a trip once," he said while he concentrated on his digging.

"Did you?"

"Yeah," he said, and dug some more, flipping little chunks of dirt onto the walk. "I don't remember it, though. I was just a baby. Me and my mom and my dad drove to somewhere. I think it was New York or somewhere."

"Don't you remember it at all?"

"Nope," Ricky said as he dislodged another piece of soil.

"Too bad."

"Yeah," he replied flatly. "I've got a picture, though. It's a picture of my dad and me."

I wondered anew about the absence of his father. "I'd like to see the picture sometime," I said.

Ricky looked up from his digging. "Would you?"

"Sure."

He dropped the stick and stood up, apparently surprised by my interest. "I have it in a book in my room. Maybe we could go over to my house and I could show it to you."

"Okay. Let's go."

He hesitated, as though he had forgotten something in his excitement. "Well, let's go see. You wait out in front for me and I'll see if it's okay if you come in."

I didn't understand why we couldn't just go into his house, but I didn't question it. "Okay," I said.

We ran across the street to Ricky's. "Wait here," he said as he bolted up the steps and into his house.

I sat on the front steps of the wood-framed house. I leaned back on my elbows and entertained myself with cloud formations that variously appeared as dogs and pigs and horse heads. My cloud musing was short-lived.

Ricky stood behind me, holding the screen door open. "You can come in now. We have to be real quiet though. My mom's . . ." His voice trailed away to an inaudible whisper. "She's real busy and we have to be quiet."

The house was smaller inside than I expected. It was sparsely furnished, and the yellowed walls were crowded with what I assumed to be pictures of ancestors—stern-faced men and unsmiling women captured in ornate wooden frames. In addition to at least a dozen of these family photos were paintings of Christ and several versions of the crucifixion. The shades in the room were drawn low, allowing little light in the room, but ineffective against the summer's heat. It was a dark, cheerless room, as still and lifeless as the photographs and paintings that occupied its walls.

"Come on," Ricky said as he hurried me through the front room to his bedroom.

Just before we entered Ricky's room, I stopped and glanced down a short hallway that led to the kitchen. Ricky's mother was sitting at a table, a large book open before her. She was moving her mouth as if to speak, though there was no sound. At the same time, she kept nodding her head in a strange rhythmic manner, as though she were displaying absolute agreement with whatever writings were in the book.

"Come on," Ricky repeated and pulled me by the arm.

Ricky's room, like the front room, was sparsely furnished. There was his metal frame bed and a two-drawer nightstand that was painted a garish green. A single lamp sat atop the nightstand. On the wall opposite his bed was a closet door covered with a full-length mirror. Attached to the wall, above the closet door, was a dust-covered crucifix. Despite the austere nature of the room, I felt he was lucky to have a real bed to sleep in, and a room that was all his.

Ricky pulled a covered cardboard box out from beneath his bed, popped the lid off the box, and anxiously removed a book from it. He held the book out at arm's length, within inches of my face. "My dad bought this book for me when I was real little. He was going to read it to me when I got bigger. It's called *Tom Sawyer*."

"I've heard of it," I said.

"Yeah," he said and pulled the book away from my face, so that he could admire the object himself. "He never got to read it to me, though," he said as he stared at the book and ran his fingers over the front cover and around the edges. "He died when I was really small. Mom says he's in heaven now. He was really nice, and smart, too."

Now I knew what Ricky had meant the day he told me he had no father. I wanted to hear more, but I was uncomfortable with Ricky's news and said nothing. I waited to see if he might cry, or tell me more about his father's death. I thought maybe he had died in the war against Hitler, or capturing a criminal, or in some terrible accident. Ricky just continued to stare silently at his treasured book, fingering it gently.

"I keep the picture in the book," he said at last.

"Can I see it?"

"Sure." He pulled a photograph out from between the pages and handed it to me without comment.

The black-and-white photo was creased and nearly separated in the lower right corner, threatening to amputate the foot of its subject—a tall, thin man in a dark suit and tie. He stood in front of an old model A Ford, cradling a bundle of white blankets that evidently contained his son. The photo had been taken at such an angle that the car and man and child looked as though they might, at any moment, tumble down the thickly treed hillside where they were gathered.

The man in the photo wore a hat and the shadow from the brim hid his eyes. He was smiling a wide, toothless smile. Only his chin, narrow and lacking any prominence, provided a visible link to the boy who now sat down next to me on the bed.

"That's me my dad is holding in the picture," Ricky said.

"Yeah, I know."

"My mom took the picture. We were either going to or coming back from somewhere," he said.

"Yeah."

"My mom let me keep the picture. She said it was mine."

We both sat and studied the picture without speaking. "This is nice to have," I said at last and handed it back to him.

"Yeah," he said as he took the photo. "I wish I could remember that trip. Sometimes at night, just before I go to sleep, I pretend my dad is still alive and that we're on a trip together. Or I pretend we're just talking or eating supper together or something. Does that seem dumb to you?"

"No," I said. I thought of all the times I had pretended my father no longer drank, and that he and my mother never fought—visions of our family without the tension that permeated our lives. "No," I repeated, "I don't think it's dumb at all."

Ricky looked at me and smiled. "Thanks."

I just smiled back and said nothing. It was then I noticed a strange transformation in his face. He looked beyond me toward the door to his room. In his eyes there was a subtle but distinct mixture of embarrassment and fear. I turned to see his mother looking down on us.

She stood in the doorway, her arms at her side. She looked rigid and pale. She appeared to be looking directly at Ricky and me, yet I had the feeling that she really didn't see us at all. It was as if she were looking through us or beyond us at some unknown point. "The Lord Jesus will forgive you," she said in a monotone.

I sat up further on the bed, in retreat from this strange pronouncement. I wanted to leave the room, but Ricky's mother blocked the only exit. I noticed that Ricky had lowered his head, bowed now toward the photograph he still clutched in his hands.

Ricky's mother clasped her hands together, but maintained her position in the doorway. "O Lord, our savior and light, help us poor sinners. Help us poor sinners."

I looked at Ricky. His head was still lowered, but I could see his face well enough to see a flush on his cheeks that was almost as red as his flaming hair.

Ricky's mother continued. "All those who accept Christ as their Lord and Savior must bow their heads and pray with me."

I bowed my head; there was nothing else I could do. As long as I had to pray, I prayed that Ricky's mother would leave the room so that I could go home.

"Bow your heads and pray with me. Bow your heads and pray with me," she repeated the words over and over.

The two of us sat on the bed, heads lowered, each trapped in his own discomfort. Ricky's mother continued to pray and chant. Her words were strange and meaningless to me. I couldn't listen or understand. I could only think of how much I wished I could escape. I kept my head down and my hands folded, and waited for her to finish. Finally, when she had apparently reached some secret level of satisfaction she simply left the room without ceremony.

Ricky looked at me, his face still flushed. "I'm sorry, Mike."

"It's okay," I said, "but I better get home now. My mom is probably wondering where I am."

"Yeah," Ricky said. "See ya."

"See ya," I said. I didn't say any more. I just left him sitting on his bed, holding his precious photograph.

I tried to explain to my mother what had happened, about how Ricky's mother had made us pray. Busy with Katy, she listened distractedly and only said that Ricky's mom must be a very religious person. She didn't seem to think there was anything peculiar about the situation. I thought I must not have explained it well enough, because I knew how wrong it had felt.

Eight

Late that summer Ron got a paper route. He delivered the evening paper six times a week and the Sunday morning paper. His route covered three entire blocks. There were ninety-eight evening papers and one hundred and twenty Sunday papers. He collected from his customers every two weeks on Thursday and Friday evenings, to pay his bill at the paper shack on Saturday morning. Whatever money remained or could be collected after he paid his bill was his to keep. With tips, he sometimes made as much as twenty dollars. It was when Ron got his route that everything began to change.

For the first several weeks, Ricky and I helped Ron deliver his evening papers. And, while my intention was to help Ron on Sundays as well, I quickly came to realize that five o'clock in the morning was too great a strain to be overcome by money or brotherhood.

On weekday afternoons, Ron walked ahead of Ricky and me as he pulled the wagon and studied his route book. We were dispatched with house-by-house orders. "Ricky, take one paper and put it inside the screen door of that yellow house," or "Mike, take one around the back and up the steps to the apartment on the right." He watched us and nodded approval as we raced back to the wagon. Within two weeks he had both the evening and Sunday routes memorized.

On the way home Ricky and I were treated to penny candy at Ralph and Jack's Grocery. There were two-cent boxes of Snaps (pieces of sugar-coated licorice), Chum Gum (three sticks for two cents), Mary Janes (a taffy candy), or miniature soda bottles made of wax and filled with brightly colored syrup. In addition to our daily diet of penny candy, we were motivated by Ron's promise to take us to the Saturday matinee at the Franklin Theater. The matinee cost ten cents and featured two movies, five cartoons, and a serial. The movies, most often, were westerns with Roy Rogers, and the serial was about G-men or Superman.

Ricky wasn't allowed to go out on Thursday or Friday evening, but I tagged along with Ron as he went from house to house collecting for the paper. Most of the people were very nice and tipped Ron a nickel or a dime, while some argued that he was collecting on the wrong week and should come back another time. Ron would insist he was there on the correct night and they would search for their last receipt stub, sometimes taking ten or fifteen minutes before they found it. They would take the stub and study the date and their calendar, finally concluding that it had, in fact, been two weeks since they had paid for the paper. Without tip or apology, they would pay as they muttered that it certainly didn't *seem* like two weeks.

Worst of all were two elderly sisters who lived in the upstairs of a duplex. They would ask Ron and me to step inside and then they would scamper around the apartment and giggle and ask us if we would like a cookie or a glass of milk. Ron always politely declined while he strained to remain patient. They would ask my age, apparently incapable of remembering the answer for more than two weeks. "And where did you get those big brown eyes?" one would ask, while her sister stood back and giggled with one hand over her mouth. "Do you have a girlfriend? What do you want to be when you grow up?" Their questions caused Ron to glare at me, as if I somehow had control of the situation. After several of these visits, Ron dubbed the two the "Terrible Gretchen Sisters" and instructed me to wait outside while he collected their payment.

Ron kept his paper route money in an old Fanny Farmer candy box. He counted the money on Thursday and Friday night to determine if he had to make early collections on Saturday morning before he went to pay his bill. On a Friday night, after we had collected and before our late dinner, Ron went to count his money once again.

I was sitting at the kitchen table, watching my mother cook, when Ron walked in holding his candy box. There was a look of shock on his face, and tiny pools of tears threatened to break and run down his cheeks. "Mom, twenty dollars of my money is missing."

Mom turned away from the stove to look at him. Her face was expressionless. "Are you sure?" she asked.

"Yeah, I'm sure. I counted it twice last night, and I counted how much me and Mike collected tonight." Now the tears came. "There's twenty dollars missing—I won't be able to pay my bill!"

Mom stared blankly at Ron and said nothing. In the warm silence of the kitchen, I heard the rolling grumble of thunder. The rumble grew and finally exploded with a deafening crack as a summer storm swept across the city. As if on cue from the thunder, Mom slammed her wooden spoon down on the stove.

"Damn him!" she said. "*Damn* him!"

Dad had been gone most of the day and just half an hour earlier had returned home in a stupor. He had said something about resting until dinner as he walked clumsily to the bedroom. Mom threw her apron on the table and marched out of the kitchen. Ron followed her, carrying his candy box. I stayed in the kitchen and smiled at Katy, who sat expectantly in her high chair. "It's okay, Katy," I said. "Mom will be right back. We'll have supper pretty soon."

I could hear yelling coming from the bedroom. Snatches of anger, punctuated with brief moments of deceptive silence. "No right . . . ," Mom shouted. "You drank it all away . . . What kind of man are you?"

I could hear the low, angry retorts of my father—not words, but waves of sound and emotion that reverberated through the tiny apartment. The sounds grew louder and angrier as they moved from bedroom to front room. I smiled at Katy, who seemed to understand that something was wrong. "It's okay, Katy. I'll be right back."

I left Katy and went to the front room. Dad stood in the middle of the room, his feet wide apart as he fumbled with the buttons on his shirt. Mom faced him, unafraid, shouting up at him. "How could you? How could you do that to your own son? He's worked so hard to make a little money."

Dad concentrated on his buttons, not looking at Mom. He gave up on his shirt and dug into his pants pockets. "Money? You want goddamn money? Here!" he shouted and threw several bills and a handful of change to the floor.

My mother, as never before, refused to retreat before my father's anger. "Damn you, Pat! You'll pay back all of it, not just a few cents left over from your stupid, drunken—"

"I'm not staying here," Dad roared. "I don't need this bull-shit. I'm going out, right now. And I'll tell you something." He leaned forward, his teeth clenched. "I'll get just as goddamn drunk as I want!"

"You bastard!" Mom spat out the words. "You'll pay back every penny. You'll pay that boy back every penny!"

I had never seen my mother display such fury. "Don't fight!" I shouted. "Please, Mom, Dad, don't fight! Please, don't fight!"

They seemed not to hear me. "Go cook your goddamn sup-per!" Dad shouted. "I'm leaving."

"Leave, you coward. Leave, and I don't really give a damn if you ever come back." In the brief silence that followed, Mom's eyes shifted from an electric anger to a watery look. It was not a look of fear, but of immeasurable sorrow. "You're killing us, Pat. Do you know that? You're killing everything I've ever felt for you."

"Aw, bullshit," Dad mumbled. He walked to the door and slammed it behind him.

Ron, still holding his candy box, stood silent. Mom hung her head dejectedly. In the kitchen, I could hear Katy crying.

I ran to the door. "Dad!" I shouted. "Come back!"

"Let him go," Mom said calmly, as if all the life and emotion had been drained out of her.

I went to the front window. From our basement view, I could only see the rain, high up, splashing off the sidewalk against the window. When the lightning flashed, I could catch a glimpse of swaying treetops and the roofs of buildings across the street bathed in the fleeting, blue-white light of the storm. "I don't see him," I said to the window.

"Come and eat, Mike," Mom said from behind me. "He'll be all right. He'll take care of himself, he always does that."

"Can I go get him?"

"He's not going anywhere," she said wearily. "He has no money."

"Maybe I should go get him for dinner," I said. I wanted my parents to be together. Perhaps if they ate together, I thought, they might reconcile. "I just want to see if he's out front."

"You can go look for him, but not out in the rain. Do you understand?"

"Yes," I said and left the apartment. I ran up the winding steps outside our door to the main entrance of the building.

He was sitting on the top step under the brick archway, looking out at the shifting ribbons of rain that swept along the street and sidewalk.

"Dad?" I said cautiously. "Are you going to eat with us?"

He looked back over his shoulder, then leaned forward, resting his elbows on his knees. "They don't want me there, Mike." The anger was gone from his voice, replaced by an unfamiliar melancholy.

"Sure they do," I said. "I do."

He didn't look back, but said something to the storm. I moved closer. "What did you say, Dad?"

"She doesn't love me," he mumbled. "Your mother doesn't love me, and your brother hates me. But you understand."

I felt angry and sick in my soul. He was wrong, and I wanted to tell him that everything would be all right if only he wouldn't drink. But I said nothing, afraid of how he might react.

"It wasn't always like this," he said, as if to himself. "I didn't always work on the road. I could have been much more. More money." He looked back at me again. "You don't remember, do you, Michael?"

A sudden gust of wind sprayed the entrance with rain. I

wiped the mist of droplets from my eyes. "Let's go eat, Dad."

"I didn't always work on the road," he said, oblivious to the storm.

"I know. Mom told us you used to be a magician."

"A musician," he said, correcting me. "I was a drummer. Damn good one, too. We used to travel all over the Midwest— even played Chicago. Cliff Stern's Rhythm Boys, featuring Pat Dougherty on the drums," he said proudly. "The dance floor would be full, all those heads bobbing to the music." His outstretched hands bounced to an unheard rhythm and visions of former glory I neither remembered nor understood. "Damn, we were good."

"Come on, Dad, let's go in."

"I might have made it to the coast—radio shows. I was that good. No more railroading Doughertys."

Somewhere above us the rain had collected and began to spill off the building in a series of splashes that struck the steps just a few feet beyond my father. "She doesn't understand what I gave up. She didn't care," he said pitifully. "No more road bands after Ron was born. Had to work steady. Get a steady job with the railroad," he said, mocking my mother's voice. Rain continued to strike the stone steps like fists of water that exploded on contact. "I could have made a big splash in this world," he said. I thought for an instant he was talking about the rain.

I heard my mother's voice call out from behind me. "Come and have your dinner before it's cold, Mike." She stood in the hallway, arms folded across her midsection. "Just leave him there, Mike."

I waited, but my father didn't say anything or look back. "Dad?" I said, but there was no response. I left him there, looking out at the rain.

Nine

"You boys hear about what happened over at Nile's Bar a while back?" Leo said as a slight grin creased his face and wrinkled the corners of his eyes.

"No sir," I said. I glanced at Ricky and hoped wildly that he would admit to nothing. His face was so ashen with fear, I thought he might faint or throw up.

Leo ran a hand through his woolly hair. "Oh, it was terrible," he said and clucked his tongue in shock and disapproval. "A terrible thing."

Ricky and I stood side by side before Leo, his ice house and chair now an outdoor courtroom and judge's bench. "A terrible thing," he repeated.

"What happened?" I said with calculated innocence.

"Well, it seems someone got up on the roof of the building and threw things down into the bar through the skylight. Buckets of water and things. It was just lucky that no one got hurt in the bar. I mean, someone could've slipped and hit their head and been hurt—even died." He shook his head in disbelief. "Can you imagine anyone doing such a darn dangerous thing?"

"No," I said. "Did they catch whoever did it?" I thought my question a masterful stroke of diversion.

Leo looked directly at me and then at Ricky. "Not yet, but maybe the police will find them. I think they send people to jail for throwing water in bars," he said. "Yeah, I'm pretty sure they do."

I heard a low moan from Ricky. "The police are looking for who did it?" I said.

"Oh, I'm pretty sure they must be. One of the fellas in the bar almost caught the ones who did it. Seems he chased them, but they got away."

"Really?"

Leo nodded. "There was three of them. Three boys about your age. He chased them over toward where you live, but they gave him the slip."

Ricky couldn't take the mounting pressure any longer. His face was as pale as it had been in the moonlight on the night of our raid. "Let's go, Mike," he said.

Leo ignored Ricky's plea. "It's a shame. You know, they probably aren't really bad kids. They're probably pretty nice fellas— like you two. I think lots of times your criminals start out that way, not really bad, just mixed up."

"What?" I said, unable to concentrate because of my fear.

"Well, my guess is that the boys who did this terrible thing are probably all confused. They probably think bars are bad places, just because people sometimes drink too much. Of course, that's wrong. It ain't the bar that's bad—or even the people who go there. It's just that some folks, well, some folks can't help drinking too much. Do you understand?"

"No," I said. I had no idea what he was trying to tell me.

Leo started over again. "Well, let's say you like ice cream, but you eat so much of it that you get sick. Now, that don't mean ice cream is bad, or that the place that sells it is bad. It just means that you, well, you don't handle ice cream very well. You see what I mean?"

"I guess so," I said. I glanced at Ricky. I could see that abstractions and analogies were lost on him, and that he could think only of getting away from all talk of police and jail.

"Well, that's what I mean. These boys are probably confused. They probably think bars are bad, just because they've seen someone get mean or sick from drinking. And, because they're all mixed up, they could end up being terrible criminals. Yeah, it's a real shame."

"Maybe they won't ever do something like that again," I said.

"Yeah," Ricky said as he came out of his state of shock. "Maybe it won't happen again."

"That would be a good thing," Leo said slowly. The faint grin left his face and he looked more serious and thoughtful. "I used to drink way too much—a long time ago. It wasn't the bar's fault, or the woman I was married to, or anyone else's fault. It was my problem. It was me. Do you understand?"

"Yes," I said.

"Well, old Leo doesn't drink at all now—not a drop. But, I don't hate bars or the people who go to them. No sir," he said emphatically, "that wouldn't be right. That wouldn't be right at all. Do you see what I'm saying?"

"Yes sir," I said, and heard echoed agreement from Ricky.

"Well, I suppose you two want to run along now," he said, smiling. Then he stood and patted both of us on top of the head with his huge paw of a hand. "Well, if the police come to see me, I'll be able to tell them that I know it ain't you two they're looking for. Yes sir, I'll be able to tell them that much for sure."

"Thanks," I said as Ricky and I turned to leave.

———

Later, I told Ron what Leo had said about the police and jail. I told him I hadn't admitted anything to Leo, or given him any hint I knew what had happened. Ron told me not to worry, and that he was almost certain the police weren't looking for us. I hoped he was right, but I felt he wasn't too sure about it himself.

Ten

On Sundays, Ron and I went to church with Mr. and Mrs. O'Neil. My mother went with Katy to early mass whenever she could, and insisted that her sons go each Sunday without fail. My father didn't say much about it, as if he were suspending judgment on the entire topic. In any event, he was often out of town on Sundays and went only with my mother's prodding when he was at home.

The O'Neils lived on the fourth floor of our building and kept pretty much to themselves. They had no children of their own and seemed to take special pleasure in having Ron and me accompany them to St. Elizabeth's Catholic Church each Sunday. Mr. O'Neil was short and plump, always calling to my mind the image of a beardless Santa Claus. He had one eye that was larger than the other, and Mom had informed me that it was made of glass. She said he had lost the eye when he was a child, the result of an accident while playing with the branch of a tree. She advised Ron and me to never play with sticks in front of him.

Mr. O'Neil drove a black Buick that he kept spotless and freshly waxed. On the way to and from church he smoked cigars, which invariably drew protests from his wife. He played Whoopee John's polka music on the car radio and ignored Mrs. O'Neil's complaints about the smoke. About halfway to St. Elizabeth's, Mrs. O'Neil always rolled down her window while she fanned the air in front of her face, and then said nothing further about the cigar.

Less than a mile east of Elliot Park, St. Elizabeth's Church beautified the corner of Fifteenth Street and Fifteenth Avenue. A small, rural-looking church, it was made of a cream-colored brick and presented a pastoral and charmingly incongruous sight in the heart of the city. The O'Neils had been married at St. Elizabeth's, and Ron had been baptized and made his first communion there. Katy and I had also been baptized at St. Elizabeth's, and now I was to begin attending weekly classes to prepare for confession and communion. The classes were being accelerated to permit completion that autumn, in order to allow for extensive repairs to the old church the following spring. This meant that confession was not far off in my future at all. I was worried about that, because I knew I would have to confess to the raid on Nile's Bar. I knew that the priest couldn't tell the police or anyone else about my confession, but the thought of the lecture and penance I was bound to receive was frightening.

Father Zimmerman was the pastor of St. Elizabeth's. I found his speech to be oddly amusing and had been told that he spoke with a German accent. He was an extraordinarily thin man, with gray-white hair that was combed straight back and slicked down. He wore wire-rimmed glasses with thick lenses and appeared in constant motion as he moved from place to place with hurried steps.

Despite Father's severe appearance and hawkish demeanor, I liked him. When he spoke with children, he was smiling and kindly and given to laughter. On the other hand, he seemed displeased with adults in general, and lashed out at them from the pulpit each Sunday in an endless litany of their weaknesses and vices. His anger and indignation grew throughout his sermon, sometimes reaching such a fever pitch that he would lapse into German, then catch himself and repeat in English what he had said. His sermons ended only when every adult head was finally hung in shame and embarrassment.

On this Sunday, as always, Father Zimmerman began slowly, explaining the meaning of the gospel he had just read. Soon he wandered into his haranguing of the parishioners. He seemed particularly unhappy. "And what does it mean to become like little children?" he boomed from the pulpit. The question lingered in the air as the parishioners fidgeted and avoided Father's penetrating gaze. "When the Lord says we must become like little children to enter the kingdom of heaven, what does that mean?"

The sun illuminated a stained glass window to my right, casting splotches of brilliant blue and red and green. The colors danced and waved across the legs of my slacks. I swung my feet back and forth beneath my seat in an alternating rhythm. The movement caused the colors to jump from leg to leg. The faster I swung my legs, the faster my rainbow leaped. I slowed the movement, then kicked out furiously, causing the colors to flicker like a multicolored flame. I felt Mrs. O'Neil gently squeeze my shoulder. She continued to look toward the altar, but held a finger to her mouth that signaled me to motionless reverence. Dimly, I heard Father Zimmerman again.

"And what of the gentle, trusting faith of children? Do you have such faith in your heart? Do people with such faith come to church on Sunday only, dressed in their finest clothes, and the rest of the week drink and fight and lie? That isn't faith. That is hypocrisy, and your sins aren't washed away because you come to church on Sunday. Sins aren't wiped clean by a bad confession, made insincere by actions. You may fool your neighbors. You may fool your friends." Father's voice grew louder, his gestures more dramatic. "You may even fool old Father Zimmerman, but you can't lie to your God or to yourself."

I watched my colors again, slowly moving one leg from side to side in a test of Mrs. O'Neil's church-misbehavior threshold.

Father Zimmerman's voice softened. "A child loves and trusts with all their heart and mind. They love without reservation, and their actions flow from that love and trust and faith. That is how you must become like children. As a child loves the parent—completely, without question or doubt. You must be obedient and trusting and faithful, as a good child. From faith of that kind comes the Christian life. A faith that is honest and innocent and free of pretense. Such a love will never be betrayed, and you must pray constantly for that kind of devotion to Jesus and his teachings."

Mrs. O'Neil nodded agreement and touched the knee of my offending leg. I gave up on my color games and sat still and silent through the rest of Father Zimmerman's sermon.

—

After church, the O'Neils treated Ron and me to ice cream at Bierman's. The four of us sat eating our cones. Ron and I answered questions about how much or little we were looking forward to school and what we had done during the week. When the O'Neils' curiosity seemed satisfied, I asked about something in the sermon that had troubled me. "What did Father Zimmerman mean when he said we should pray all the time?" I asked.

The O'Neils looked at each other over their cones, debating with their eyes who should answer my question. Mr. O'Neil sat back and took time to wipe his mouth with his napkin. "It's good to know you listened to the sermon, Michael. Some children don't always listen." He smiled.

"But, what did he mean?" I persisted.

Mr. O'Neil noisily cleared his throat and glanced at his wife. "I don't think he said that, exactly, did he?"

Mrs. O'Neil narrowed her eyes, as if her husband were an inattentive student. "He said that we should pray constantly. That is what he said," she said with authority.

"Yes," Mr. O'Neil said, "that's what he said. He said we should pray constantly—and, of course, we should."

I sat and waited for Mr. O'Neil to continue, but we just quietly stared at each other. I noticed his ample cheeks were flushed, and his glass eye appeared to grow larger.

"The boy wants to know what he meant by that," Mrs. O'Neil said.

"Well, what he meant is that we should always be the very best person we can be, and we should pray whenever we get the chance. Yes, that's probably what he meant."

"But, does it mean that we should pray all day long? I mean, isn't it enough to pray at night when you go to bed, and in church on Sunday?"

Ron looked at me with disdain. "Nobody can pray all the time," he said. "That's stupid. You couldn't get anything else done if all you did was go around praying all the time."

"Your brother is right," Mr. O'Neil said. "A person can't be praying all the time. Why, if they did that they couldn't work or play or go to school and study or talk like we're doing now."

"But what about if you're at a friend's house and their mother prays out loud and wants you to pray, too? Is that what you should do? I mean, is that the way a person should be?" I said.

Mr. O'Neil looked puzzled. "What do you mean, Michael?"

Now I began to wish I hadn't asked. I didn't want to tell about Ricky's mom in any detail; it felt to me that somehow that would be a betrayal of Ricky. "Just, if someone—like an adult— if they pray out loud and ask you to pray with them, is that what Father Zimmerman thinks a person should do?"

At first, my clarification appeared to do nothing but further mystify Mr. O'Neil. But after a moment of reflection, he suddenly brightened. "If you live as you should—keep the commandments, be nice to your parents and your brother and your sister—that is your prayer. I believe that is what Father Zimmerman meant. You see, your behavior—your life—becomes a prayer. And as you live, you pray constantly," he said. He looked at his wife and they exchanged smiles. Mr. O'Neil seemed extraordinarily proud of himself. "There, does that answer your question?"

"I guess so," I said, though it didn't answer my real question at all. It was a question I could not state clearly. It was a question that, to me, in a frightening, unthinkable way was aimed at the heart of all authority and sacred beliefs.

Eleven

Summer ended in a series of exhaustingly hot, tedious August days. Other than helping Ron with his paper route, there were afternoons when Ricky and I found nothing more pressing or imaginative to do than sit on the curb and lift bubbled wads of sun-cooked tar from the edge of the street with our Popsicle sticks. There was a brief flicker of hope that Ron and I might go to the state fair with our parents, but there were problems with money and the plans simply faded and died away.

A week or so before school, my mother and Ron and I walked to Kaplan Brothers Factory Outlet Store on Franklin Avenue and bought clothes for the new school year—two pairs of jeans for each of us, six flannel shirts in brightly colored plaids, and one pair of Buster Brown shoes for me. Ron helped pay for most of his own clothing with money saved from his route, and even treated Mom and me to a Coke on the way home. Mom thanked Ron and smiled at him with her mouth and eyes and told him she could see that he was growing up to be a fine young man.

School began inauspiciously, with Ricky assigned to Mrs. Mitchell's class and me to the dreaded Miss Tremble's room. Within the first week, however, I found a balance to Ricky's absence and a sort of ineffable exhilaration that made Miss Tremble's stern, humorless authority bearable. With students arranged alphabetically by last name, I found myself sitting directly behind Lisa Delaney. Lisa Delaney—petite, magnetic, ostensibly reticent, whose golden hair cascaded down to her shoulders where it nestled in ringlets on her dress. Lisa Delaney, who had mastered a strange contortion that allowed her to bend backward in a seated position until her golden hair was fanned out across my desk top, her eyes rolled up in her head so that she could look out over her eyebrows at me. "Hi, Mike," she'd say in a whisper.

"Hi! I hope your hair doesn't fall in my inkwell."

Lisa didn't flinch. "Don't let it. You can touch it, if it's near your inkwell."

"It's okay," I'd say nervously. "I think it'll be okay."

Lisa told me she found most boys to be mean and silly, but I was different. She also told me where she lived and that maybe she could walk with Ricky and me to school, since her house was on our way. I told her that would be great with me, if we happened to see each other. After that, I made sure Ricky and I lingered in front of Lisa's house until she joined us on the way to school. With three of us, there was less chance of being teased by other boys about liking a girl. And there was a faint stirring, some new, indescribable lightness in having a girl with golden hair walk with you and tell you how much she liked you.

For me, fall became an exciting rebirth after the oppressive heat that had ended the summer. It had a freshness greater than spring. There was Lisa and the morning air, which became nose-running cold and quickened your step and appetite. On the way to school, until we reached Lisa's house, Ricky and I would join other boys who ran alongside the ragpickers' wagons, taunting them as they called out for rags and old metal. Playing their role in the autumn ritual, the old ragpickers ignored us as they sat atop their open wooden wagons that were pulled lethargically by a single aging horse.

In the wind, the fallen leaves scratched and cartwheeled along the avenue, and the steps of the entrance to our building were now devoid of the gatherings of people who had idled away so many hours watching the passing of the summer months. In the evenings, the air was heavy with the smell of leaves that had been raked into piles and set afire at curbside.

It impressed me as a season of hope and new beginnings. Most of all, there was my father. He had had nothing to drink for over two months and had repaid Ron the route money he had taken. There were pleasant evenings at home now. There were nights when my parents hugged, and now and then the sound of laughter in our house. Ron had abandoned much of his previous surliness, and at night, when Dad was on the road, I could hear Mom and Ron talking in the kitchen about Christmas gifts they wanted to buy and how much money they could save.

This feeling of well-being went unabated until the day I made Miss Tremble smile. The day began well enough, with no indication of the difficulty ahead. After the Pledge of Allegiance, Miss Tremble wanted to talk about the upcoming election. "Can anyone tell us the names of the two men running for president?"

Several hands went into the air, including my own.

"Michael Dougherty," Miss Tremble said, "please stand up

and tell the class the names of the candidates."

Lisa turned in her seat to look up at me and smile. "Harry Truman and Thomas Dewey," I said proudly.

"Very good, Michael. Now, can you tell us something about each of them?"

I was stuck. It was unfair. I had answered her question, only to be asked another before I could take my seat. I looked at Lisa, who broadened her smile. I looked at Miss Tremble, who stared back at me impassively. I watched the clock above the blackboard until the minute hand jumped forward to an ominously loud *click*. Then, inspiration struck as I remembered something my father had said. "Well, I think the newspapers and radio are all wrong. They say Dewey is going to win, but I think Truman will win because he's for the working man. Dewey isn't really saying anything at all. He just smiles and looks like the little man on top of a wedding cake."

To my amazement, Miss Tremble grinned and then pretended to cough to keep from laughing. "Well," she said as she turned away from the class. "Yes, well, that is very interesting, Michael. Thank you. You may take your seat now."

"You're so smart," Lisa said and smiled at me and shook her golden hair.

———

Ricky waited for Lisa and me on the southeast corner each day, then the three of us would cross Park Avenue together and head home. As Lisa and I walked across the playground to our rendezvous, I saw a circle of students on the corner. The circle was six or seven people deep, with those in the back springing into the air to get a better look at what was taking place at the center. There was no mistaking this kind of after-school crowd—it was a fight.

I hurried toward the corner. "Come on, Lisa, let's see what's going on."

Lisa slowed her pace. "It's a fight. They're stupid."

"Come on," I shouted over my shoulder and sprinted to the corner without her.

When I reached the circle, I joined the bobbing spectators at the perimeter. I placed my hands on the shoulders of the boy in front of me and leaped into the air. On my first jump I was only able to identify one of the fighters—Larry Olson. Larry was one grade ahead of me, and known for his delight and prowess at administering schoolyard thrashings. He was also known for his obesity, outweighing any other student at Madison by at least twenty pounds. Larry's method of defeating his opponents was well known. He would charge, using his enormous size to knock his victims to the ground. Once they were on their back, Larry sat on them, pinning them helplessly to the ground with his great bulk. One deft swing with his right hand and the opponent's nose was bloodied and the fight was over. Of course, all of this was preceded by insults and taunting to anger his enemy.

I jumped again. The fight had not yet begun, and now I knew I had to find a way to stop it. The object of Larry's hostility was Ricky.

I pushed my way through the crowd until I burst into the area cleared for the fight. At closer range, Larry looked far more menacing than he had from outside the circle.

"I don't like you, kid," Larry snarled.

Ricky said nothing.

"I don't like the way you act and I don't like your orange hair," he said and took two steps toward Ricky. Ricky retreated, and as the crowd fell silent for a moment, I could hear the *zirp-zirp* of his corduroy pants as he backed away.

"I hear your mother is crazy, kid. I hear she walks around and talks to herself. She got orange hair, too?" He pushed Ricky's shoulders.

I could see that Ricky was about to cry. His face was flushed and tears were gathering in his eyes. I knew what Larry was about to do, and I knew I had to stop him somehow. I could feel my knees shaking as I stepped farther into the circle. "Leave him alone, fat-ass!" I shouted.

Larry wheeled around to face me. "What'd you say?"

"I said leave him alone."

Larry advanced toward me. "Who's gonna make me?"

"My brother," I said.

"Yeah, and who's your brother?"

"Ron Dougherty. He's in junior high and he's bigger and tougher than you are." I hoped desperately that my ploy would work.

"Never heard of him," Larry said. "Now what did you call me, kid?"

I didn't want to repeat the insult, afraid that my beating would be all the more severe. "Why don't you pick on someone your own size?" I said.

Larry came closer. "What did you call me, huh?"

I backed up. "I didn't call you anything," I said.

"Yes, you did, you little twerp. Now, what did you call me, huh?" he repeated and shoved me back by the shoulders.

"Why don't you pick on someone your own size?" I said again, hoping to appeal to his pride.

"I'll pick on anyone I want," he said and shoved me again.

I could see that I had truly enraged him. Larry didn't need to invent a reason to justify trouncing me. My slur on his size had been an incredible mistake. Then the great surge came. In a blur of stomach and elbows and hands, the earth moved out from beneath me and I found myself on my back. Larry stood over me. "You're gonna get it now, you little twerp!"

Larry inched forward slightly, so that his feet straddled my rib cage. He was about to take his seat on me, to execute one or more blows to my face. The prospect was unbearable, and in my panic I did the only thing that seemed to offer some hope of escape. I grabbed his ankles and, using them for leverage, rolled back on my shoulders. I kicked out with my right foot as hard and quickly as I could. The heel of my shoe landed with a sickening thud between Larry's legs, and it felt for an instant as if he were lifted off the ground. I heard him gasp and saw him grab at his crotch with both hands. He tottered backward several paces, then fell to the ground and curled up, snail-like. He squirmed and moaned and held himself between the legs. "Oh shit, oh God," he repeated over and over as he writhed on the ground.

I got up and ran to Ricky. "Let's get out of here," I said and grabbed him by the arm. "Come on, quick, before he gets up." Ricky said nothing, but turned to leave with me as the crowd silently parted to let us pass.

Lisa stood at the edge of the crowd. There was no hint of kindness or admiration in her eyes—only disappointment and revulsion. "That was icky, Mike. That was really icky."

"I couldn't help it," I said.

Lisa twisted away from me, spinning in a leave-me-alone pivot, her golden hair flashing in the sun. She refused to walk with us, maintaining a proper distance behind Ricky and me. Ricky was much less discriminating about the manner in which Larry had been defeated. He thanked me for my help.

We hurried toward home, with me looking back periodically

to see Lisa, who looked away, and to see if Larry was after us. My legs were still shaking and my thoughts raced to previously unknown corners of fear and shame. In one foolish, desperate action I had destroyed Lisa's feelings for me—had exposed myself as an odious creature. And alternating with that thought was the realization that I would eventually pay a terrible price for what I had done to Larry. He would recover and find me. What might happen to me then was too horrible to contemplate.

Twelve

The months that led to Christmas characterized life's vagaries. Nothing seemed predictable. Larry did not seek retribution. In fact, when I was no longer able to avoid encountering him in the school hallways, I was surprised by a greeting that wavered somewhere between friendliness and indifference. My hours of anguish had been without foundation. It was as if our fight had never taken place. On the other hand, the intensity of Lisa's feelings for me—both affection and disapproval—simply vanished. She no longer walked to school with Ricky or me, and displayed a keen new interest in Andrew Bojelski, who sat across the aisle from her and spent most of the school day passing her notes. My desktop was never again adorned by her flaxen hair.

Confession, too, went essentially without incident. I had agonized over how I could possibly confess to both the raid on Nile's Bar and my shameful assault on Larry. I even considered not confessing to the acts at all, but knew that such omissions would only plunge me into a deeper state of moral decay. In the end, out of a fear of eternal damnation that was greater than my fear of penance, I told it all. Except for one or two clarifying questions, and a brief judgment that I was right to do what I could to help a threatened friend, but wrong to attack Larry as I had, there was no stern lecture. There was no evidence of shock or dismay or unprecedented horror on the part of the priest. There was nothing said at all about Nile's Bar, and a penance of just two Our Fathers and three Hail Marys. I left the confessional feeling relieved and content and full of grace.

The following Sunday, dressed in a new pair of navy blue slacks and a white shirt, I made my first communion. My father was on the road and unable to attend, but the O'Neils and my mother and Ron and Katy were there. I received a card and two dollars from Grandma Dougherty, my only surviving grandparent, and a card and a dollar from Aunt Marie, my mother's older sister. After church, everyone came to our apartment and there was cake for all of us and a gift to me from the O'Neils. It was a ceramic statue of a boy kneeling to receive communion from Christ.

The card from my aunt Marie had a note that said she would see us all at Christmas. Aunt Marie lived in the western Minnesota town of Alexandria and taught school. She had never married, and had taken care of her and Mom's parents during the last years of their lives—years wracked by debilitating illness and depression. After they died, she said she had had her fill of taking care of people. She didn't need or want a man so badly that she would jeopardize her freedom and independence by marrying. Her life was full but uncomplicated, and that is how she wished it to remain. At first, I believe Mom thought Aunt Marie's attitude was selfish or, at best, a terrible mistake. But, with the passage of years, she had grown to respect her sister's unorthodox view and even found virtue in her honesty.

Though separated in age by ten years, my mother and her older sister clearly shared the most intense bond. When Marie stayed with us, the two of them sat in our tiny kitchen and drank tea and talked late into the night, their voices hushed to keep from disturbing the rest of us. The buzz of their conversations was punctuated with muffled laughter and signs of affection. And, at least once whenever Aunt Marie visited us there would be an excursion to downtown Minneapolis on the streetcar. She would insist on taking us all to lunch at the Forum Cafeteria, and over my mother's protests, Marie would buy her a new dress or blouse.

I always enjoyed Aunt Marie's visits, not just because of her generosity, but because of her energy and enthusiasm for life, and her ability to bring some happiness to my mother. With Ron and me there were bear hugs and kisses on the forehead and puzzles and games of her own creation. "What's missing from this house?" she'd say after drawing furiously. When I answered "the chimney" or "a window" or "a doorknob" there was praise and hugs and mischievous winks and smiles.

Whether her physical appearance was a consequence or a reflection of her attitude seems a point of unanswerable debate. While she and my mother shared a stature of just five feet, and liquescent brown eyes of extraordinary alertness and emotion, Marie had a certain robust presence that made Mom appear fragile in comparison. Heavier, sturdier, her dark hair cut short and streaked with gray, Marie was not pretty, she was handsome.

I didn't understand my father's response to Aunt Marie. When she stayed with us he spoke with her very little and retreated into a dark, brooding silence, as if he could not or would not share in my mother's pleasure with Marie's visit. I never heard him say anything critical of her, but I couldn't help noticing how often he absented himself from her company, finding reasons to go for walks or make an extra run on the road or simply sit and listen to the radio while my mother and Marie visited in the kitchen. After she left, he seemed relieved, as if he had regained a lost position of eminence in his own home.

—

Aunt Marie was scheduled to arrive in Minneapolis exactly one week before Christmas. Mom spent an entire day cleaning our tiny apartment and offering assurances that a cot set up across the room from the couch would be just fine for me. Aunt Marie could sleep on the couch, which afforded an adult a little more comfort and space than a cot. Katy's crib could remain in my parents' bedroom, and Ron's space—a curtained-off section of the bedroom—could also remain undisturbed. In her nervous anticipation, Mom repeatedly assured me that the cot would not be a problem for me, and I repeatedly agreed that it was okay.

That evening at dinner, Dad followed his usual course and became withdrawn and silent. He mumbled inarticulate responses to my mother's excitement about Marie's impending arrival. When he had finished eating he announced that he was going to walk to Franklin Avenue to buy a Christmas tree.

"Can't you wait until tomorrow, or at least until after Marie gets here?" Mom asked.

"Do you want a tree or not?" he snarled.

Mom said nothing. She just rose from her chair and smiled thinly at Ron and me and asked us to help clear the dishes. She didn't say anything more until my father was ready to leave. "Try not to be too long," she called after him. The only response was the sound of the door being slammed.

Marie arrived by taxi at eight-thirty, with a suitcase and a shopping bag brimming with colorfully wrapped gifts. Her entrance, as always, was verbal as well as physical. Between hugs, she kept up a constant patter about her fellow passengers on the Greyhound that ran from Alexandria to Minneapolis. The cast of characters might have stepped right out of a Jack Benny radio show. Eccentric, hapless, neurasthenic people were paraded before us in Marie's account of her trip. The story went on while Mom took Marie's coat and suitcase and bag of gifts. Then, abruptly, the story ended and Marie held my mother by the shoulders at arm's length. "God, it's good to see you, honey."

"It's good to see you, too," Mom said.

They stood there, looking at one another like lost children who have finally been reunited after a cruel, enforced separation. Then they hugged. Marie patted my mother on the back and stroked her hair and whispered. "How have you been?"

Mom leaned back, still within the circle of Marie's arms. "I've been just fine."

"And the baby?"

My mother smiled. "Katy's asleep. Wait till you see her. She's a little beauty. Just an angel."

Aunt Marie released her grip on Mom and turned toward Ron and me. "I'm not surprised," she said. She leaned toward us, her hands on her knees. "Just look at these two handsome fellows. Ron, you're as tall as I am, and your mother tells me you're a terrific student."

"Thanks," Ron said. He blushed faintly and lowered his head.

"And here's my sweetie. How are you, Michael?" she said and chucked me under the chin.

"I'm fine," I said.

"I love you boys, and I've missed you both." She winked at us and straightened up and turned toward Mom again. "And where's Pat?"

"He should be home anytime now. He wanted so much to be here when you arrived, but he had to walk down to Franklin to get a tree."

"How's he been?" Aunt Marie asked.

"He's been great, really. Why the last few months, it's been . . . he's been wonderful." Mom glanced nervously at Ron and me, her face etched with discomfort. "Why don't you boys get in your pajamas and look at some comics. Your aunt Marie and I want to have some tea and talk."

"But Mo—" Ron began to object.

"Do as your mother says," Marie cut him off. "There'll be plenty of time to visit with your old aunt. I'll be here all week."

Ron muttered something to himself, but returned an embrace proffered by Aunt Marie. The two of us settled onto the couch, dismissed from the adult world, but near enough to them to feel a part of the warmth that had enveloped our tiny home.

Ron and I were only halfway through our first comic when there was a scratching sound followed by two hollow thumps at the door. I saw Mom spring from her chair in the kitchen. "That must be Pat now," she said to Marie. "Boys," she called to us, "open the door for your father. He may need some help with the tree."

Ron and I raced to the entrance. When the door was opened, the entire space was filled with spruce tree. From somewhere behind the dark green expanse I could hear my dad's voice. "Ron, you and Mike get hold of the bottom of the tree and pull it into the house."

Pine needles showered onto the floor and hallway of the building as we grappled with the tree. Once it was inside, Dad held the tree at its center and stood it upright. A single long shoot of pine that topped the tree nearly touched the ceiling. "I'll have to cut a little off, but isn't it a beauty? I must have looked at a hundred trees before I found this one."

"I was starting to worry," Mom said. "You were gone so long. But, it's a wonderful tree, Pat," she added quickly. Then, more formally she said, "Pat, Marie is here. She's been here nearly an hour."

"Hello, Pat," Marie said.

Dad only glanced toward her and turned back to the tree. "Marie," he said brusquely. And in the instant it took him to speak that single word, I came to realize that my father had not spent all his time in search of a Christmas tree. Mingled with the smell of pine and hot tea was the distinct, sour smell of alcohol on his breath. But there was only that frightening odor, no anger or reckless accusations, and my hope was that whatever he had had to drink would not spoil the evening or Marie's visit.

"Get me my saw and the tree stand," Dad commanded no one in particular. Then the torturous process began.

"I'm going to cut a little off the trunk and snip the top. Ron, you and Mike hold this thing steady while I saw a piece off the bottom." He rested the tree on the floor, then called for books to place beneath the base of the pine. Mom, anticipating him, handed him several books almost as soon as he had asked.

Ron and I grasped the thick base of the tree as Dad began to saw. Each time he drew back the blade, the rough trunk rolled and scraped our hands. "Put your weight on the goddamn thing," Dad said. "Ron, put some weight on it with your knee." Ron did as he was told, as I struggled ineffectually to help hold the tree steady.

When a column of wood perhaps four inches long had been removed from the base, Dad lifted the tree and dropped it into the stand. He tightened the bolts on the stand, then stood up to examine his work. He stepped back a few feet. The tree began to lean to the right, then suddenly left its base, about to topple to the floor. Dad bolted forward and caught the tree as it neared a forty-five degree angle to the floor. He pulled it out of the stand with excessive force and wrestled the monster tree up against the wall. He knelt down next to the stand and swore at it. It was then that my mother had the temerity to ask if she and Marie might help him in some way.

Dad, his face flushed with resentment, looked up from where he squatted next to the tree stand. "Fine," he said and stood up. He held the tree stand by one of its three metal legs. "You want to try and put the goddamn thing up, be my guests. Maybe Marie has some goddamn clever way of getting it to stand up in a broken piece of crap like this."

"Pat!" Mom said, her voice betraying her embarrassment.

"Don't 'Pat' me," my father bellowed. "You can fix the son of a bitch. You're so goddamn smart!" He looked down at the stand that dangled from his hand, the stand he never replaced but that year after year frustrated his attempts to master it. He pitched the stand, backhand, into a corner of the room. "I'm going out," he said. "Don't bother to wait up for me."

None of us moved or said a word as he gathered up his coat and gloves and left the apartment. Any movement, any sound, could only add to the tension.

In his wake, the four of us spent the next hour struggling to set up the big, undecorated failure of a Christmas tree. When it was finally in place before the front window, Mom ushered Ron and me off to bed and returned to the kitchen with Aunt Marie. From my cot I could smell freshly steeped tea and hear my mother and her sister talking.

"I'm sorry about Pat," Mom said. "It's just that he's so tense. I mean, things like the tree are very upsetting to him."

"He'd been drinking," Marie said, unwilling to be part of any pretense about her brother-in-law's sensitivities.

There was a prolonged silence, broken only by the hissing sound of tea being sipped and tested. "He may have had a drink or two," Mom said at last.

"Look," Marie said, and in her voice I could sense that she was leaning forward, exploiting the unique bond the two of them shared. "I've never told you how to live your life, and God knows I've never listened to anyone who wanted to tell me how to live mine, but don't lie to yourself. The man has always had some real problems. One of those problems is liquor."

"But Marie, he's been so wonderful these past months."

"Don't," Marie said. She spoke with a steady, reassuring strength—low, rich sounds of honesty and confidence. "Don't make excuses for him. Look, honey, you know I'm not a meddler. I've watched and kept silent for years. I've always felt that it wasn't my place to criticize or interfere with your relationship with Pat, but you've got the kids to think about, too. The boys are getting older now. They understand what's going on. Did you see their faces when Pat blew up tonight?"

"No," my mother said weakly.

"Well, I did. Ron looked so angry I thought he was going to attack his own father, and Mike was so frightened it nearly brought me to tears. Is that what you're willing to put them through? Is that the sort of home you want them to have?"

"You know it isn't." My mother's voice strengthened, an edge to it now.

"Just a minute," Marie said, and I heard her walk to my cot. "Michael?" she whispered. "Michael, are you asleep?"

I didn't answer. In a moment I heard her head back to the kitchen.

"Don't be angry with me, please," Marie said. "It isn't easy for me to say these things. It isn't something I take pleasure in doing. And maybe you won't want me around when I'm done saying what I have to say, but, by God, I'll say it anyway."

"No one is ever going to throw you out," Mom said, "but you really don't know Pat as I do."

"Maybe. Maybe you're right," Marie said, "but I'll tell you what I *do* know, and what breaks my heart. Honey, most of all it breaks my heart to see you treated so badly by someone I know you love so much. I watch, and I understand, and I know that you hope—you believe—that somehow things will change. That Pat will stop drinking and give back all the caring and tenderness you've brought to him over the years. You believe that someway, somehow, he'll wake up one morning and appreciate all you do and all you've done for him. He'll look around and really see what a beautiful family you've given him. You believe that and hope for that and pray for that, don't you?"

From the kitchen I could hear strange sounds, and then Mom's voice choking out a response. "Yes, I do," she said.

"Well, honey, I don't think you can count on that." Marie's voice grew softer, and I could hear only words and phrases. "People don't treat the ones they love like that . . . sick . . . as if you were nothing . . . the boys know . . ."

"For better or for worse, that was the vow I took. What are you telling me to do?" My mom sounded defeated and confused.

"He took some vows, too. And loving someone doesn't mean you give them license to mistreat you, or stand back and do nothing to keep them from destroying themselves and everyone around them. At some point, you're going to realize that. All the vows and loyalty and caring in the world won't justify the scars these children will carry all their lives if you allow this to continue."

My mother was crying freely now, unable or unwilling to suppress emotions that had been held in check for so long.

They continued to talk, but I didn't listen. I didn't understand all of what they had said, but the essence of their conversation was clear to me. On my cot, in the sweet-smelling darkness, I was crying now, too. I looked across the room at our huge, impossible tree and wept with my mother and for my mother, and for all of the unfathomable, desperate ugliness of our lives.

Thirteen

Marie stayed until the day after Christmas. The incident with the tree had cast a shadow on her visit, but my father stayed sober for the rest of her time with us, and by Christmas morning we had all settled into a sort of stilted holiday spirit. Ron's gifts helped. With his route money he had gotten everyone a present, including Dad. He gave Aunt Marie a lavender-scented sachet, barrettes to Mom, and a new shaving mug for our father. He gave Katy a wooden duck on wheels that rose and fell like a horse on a merry-go-round as it was pulled across the floor by a long red string attached to its bill. Other than the sight of a streetcar, I'd never seen anything that thrilled her as much as that duck. And for me there was an ornately decorated cap gun. Along the barrel of the gun, amid stamped swirls and curlicues, was the word *Grizzly*. The plastic plates on the handle of the gun were ivory-colored and imprinted with the growling head of a grizzly bear.

There were other gifts, of course—more practical things. There were pajamas for us from Aunt Marie, and socks and shirts and even a shoeshine kit from my parents. But the presents Ron gave were extraordinary. He had worked so hard and been so thoughtful in his gift selection that I think each of us was touched in a very special way. Katy, with a little prompting from my mother, gave Ron two hugs and announced that she loved her duck forever.

—

During the second week of our Christmas vacation, after Marie had gone, I spent most of my time with Ricky. His Christmas, though not marred by any emotional crisis, sounded more somber than ours. More accurately, it sounded as if he had had no Christmas at all. As we sat together on the couch in my apartment late one afternoon, Ricky gave only the most abbreviated answers to my questions as he admired Ron's gift to me.

"Did you and your mom have any company for Christmas?"

"Nope," Ricky said as he ran his fingers along the barrel of my cap gun. He turned the gun around and studied the head of the grizzly bear that decorated the handle.

"My aunt Marie stayed with us. She's really swell."

"Yeah," Ricky said as he held the gun, shooting-style, and pointed it across the room at some imaginary villain.

"What'd you get for Christmas?"

"Just stuff," he said as he leaned back deep into the couch, one eye closed to take more careful aim at his enemy.

"Me too, mostly. Stuff like shirts and pajamas. My cap gun is the best gift I got."

"Yeah," he said and turned toward me. "You're really a lucky stiff." His eyes widened. "Can we get some caps and shoot it?"

"I don't have any caps, and I can't shoot it in the house." Ricky was disappointed. "But, this summer we can get caps, and

I'll let you use it sometimes, too."

He brightened. "Really?"

"Sure. Maybe we could help Ron with his route and get some money and buy another gun, too."

"Yeah," he said, his eyes distant and dreamy with the dazzling prospect of cap gun fights in the spring. Then his face darkened. "I'll never have a gun this nice though," he said matter-of-factly as he handed the pistol back to me.

"Maybe," I said, "we could find out where Ron got it and you could save up and get one, too."

"Naw." He dismissed the possibility with a shrug of his tiny shoulders. "It's okay. I'll just never have one that nice."

———

We played for a while outside, before the clear light of the winter afternoon began to fade to a blue-black evening. By five o'clock Ron had returned from his route and Ricky and I were back indoors warming ourselves with mugs of hot chocolate. My mother invited Ricky to join us for dinner. At his insistence, she phoned his mother for approval and found out that he could stay with us, but had to be home no later than seven.

As we finished a meal of homemade soup and hamburgers, Ron looked across the table at Ricky and me and smiled thinly. "You two want to go outside for a while?"

"I think we're going to look at some comics. Besides, our jackets are probably still wet and it's cold out," I said.

"Aw, come on," Ron said, "don't be a sissy. The three of us can go out, it's not that cold." He widened his eyes, then furrowed his brow as he motioned with his head toward the door. It was a signal of some clandestine plan.

"Hey, Mom, is it okay if me and Mike and Ricky play outside for a while?"

"Yes," she said, without turning from the sink to look at us. "Just be sure that you don't wander off. Remember, Ricky has to be home by seven."

Ron smiled broadly and flashed his signal again. "See, it's okay. Come on, let's go out for a little bit."

Ricky and I looked at each other. Ricky gave me a nod of approval. "Okay," I said.

After we had wrestled our way into damp jackets and stocking hats and left the building, Ron revealed his secret. "The streets are perfect for car hopping. I noticed it on the way home from my route."

Ricky turned to me for explanation. He said nothing, but his face was a stark question mark.

Car hopping was a free winter sport conducted only under cover of darkness on residential streets. Roads had to be icy. You waited twenty or thirty feet from a corner with a stop sign. You remained in hiding, preferably behind a large snowbank, until you spotted a car slowing to a stop. Then, crouching and moving quickly up behind the car, you grabbed the bumper before the car pulled away. You could sometimes slide behind the car two or three blocks until the next stop. There were, of course, hazards. Positioning yourself behind the exhaust pipe invariably shortened your ride, as did patches of dry pavement.

"Remember," Ron said, "you can't hit the car hard or the driver will hear you. If he hears you, he'll chase you."

"What do they do if they catch you?" Ricky said, his voice crackling with excitement and fear.

"I don't know, I've never been caught. Just kind of slide up to the car, and don't touch anything but the bumper. Okay?"

"Okay," Ricky and I said in unison.

The three of us stationed ourselves behind a snowbank, needlessly whispering in the bitter wind. "Remember," Ron said, "we keep low and run after the car when I say so."

"Okay," I said.

Ricky just nodded, and I could hear his teeth clicking in response to the chill of the night. After only three or four minutes I was already discouraged by the cold. "Ron, my feet are freezing. Let's go in. I don't think there are going to be any cars tonight."

"Don't be chicken. Come on."

At that moment, a Chevy coupe came into sight and began to slow down.

"This is it," Ron said excitedly. "Get ready, you guys."

On his command, we raced toward the car as it rolled to a stop. Ron reached the Chevy first, executing a silent attachment to its bumper. I was next, managing a successful, if not as graceful, maneuver. Ricky, in his novice enthusiasm, forgot to slow his stride as he neared the car. Just as it began to pull away, he struck the rear of the vehicle with both mitten-clad hands. There was a hollow *thunk* and the car stopped abruptly. I could hear the car door open and Ron shouting for us to run.

"What the hell's going on?" the driver's voice boomed. "You kids get the hell away from this car!"

We ran, our sure-footed speed inspired by panic. We had gone nearly half a block when we realized that we weren't being chased. Evidently the driver had decided pursuit over the treacherous street and walks simply wasn't justified. Ron immediately began to lobby Ricky and me to give it another try. Predictably, we returned to our hiding place to await another opportunity.

Ricky was excited, warmed now by his own enthusiasm. "I can do it, Ron. Really, the next car that comes—I can do it." He spoke with uncharacteristic resolve, his words coming out in great puffs of vapor that rose and vanished in the clear night air.

"I know you can, Ricky. It just takes a little practice. You'll be fine," Ron said.

In moments, our second chance appeared in the form of a black Ford sedan. As before, we darted out on Ron's command. This time each of us managed to secure a space on the rear bumper, our timing a matter of professional excellence. Unfortunately, my spot was directly behind the tailpipe.

We crossed the intersection and headed south toward Franklin Avenue. Ron had been right, the street was perfect. Our boots moved smoothly over the glazed street. It was car hopping at its very best, our bodies moving as one with the Ford. But the fumes from the exhaust became too much for me, and before we crossed the next intersection I released my grip on the bumper and glided to a halt. I stood and watched Ron and Ricky and the Ford disappear into the dark corridor of the street. I ran to the sidewalk and jogged toward Franklin to meet them.

After the Ford had stopped and then turned left onto Franklin, I saw Ron and Ricky headed toward me on the sidewalk. I could hear Ron praising Ricky as they approached. "Mike!" Ron called out when he spotted me in the darkness, "you should have seen Ricky. He was great, just great." He clapped Ricky on the back. "He rode it even longer than me. He stayed with it all the way to the corner—hung on till the thing stopped."

"Yeah? Way to go, Ricky," I said. "I would've stayed with you guys, but I was choking to death on the exhaust."

The three of us headed home, Ricky flanked by Ron and me. He said little other than "Thanks" as we congratulated him on his skill and courage. As we walked along, Ricky appeared to grow taller—buoyed up by his own success and our recognition.

In those few minutes, I know that Ricky felt closer to us than ever before, and no doubt cherished Ron's shortened, more manly version of his name as we parted. "So long, Rick," Ron shouted as Ricky crossed the street to head home.

"See ya, Ron. See ya, Mike," he called out triumphantly.

I watched my friend cross the icy, snow-covered street and then break into a joyous sprint toward his house. I watched him until he was beyond the glow of the streetlight, until his figure was no more than a shadowy movement amid the bluish-white mounds of snow that lined the avenue.

Fourteen

Two days before our Christmas vacation was to end, the Minnesota winter turned unseasonably warm. Beneath the distant, low-arcing sun, the temperature climbed above the freezing mark, transforming the icy streets into rutted, brownish slush. The mounds of snow that bordered and defined the avenue receded, gathering a gray mire at their tops. This brief reprieve from the bitter cold was not winter at its most pristine and picturesque, but it was ideal for snowball fights and building fortresses and snowmen. It was that short interlude when winter holds its breath and allows a nostalgic hint of spring.

Behind our building, in an empty lot that spanned the width of two backyards, Ricky and I worked diligently on a snow fort that promised to be impregnable. Though not entirely by design, our fort had become a labyrinth of hallways and anterooms and secret chambers. As our creation grew, we invented a purpose for every new wall and compartment.

"If they come in here," Ricky said, referring to any potential invaders who might enter the main room of our fort, "we could run back there." He swung around and pointed a soggy red mitten in the direction of a narrow break in a wall that led to another room. "We could have snowballs back there, and if they chased us, we'd be ready for them."

"Yeah," I said. I stopped packing slush on a wall and stood to survey our meandering structure. It was a thing of intricate beauty, standing no higher than three feet at any point. I studied it carefully and marveled at what we had accomplished. "We could have snowballs in every room. Nobody could ever beat us in a snowball fight."

"Yeah," Ricky said as he joined me in admiring our handiwork.

"I've never seen as good a fort," I said.

"But we could make it even better."

"How?"

"We could put a roof on it."

"A roof?"

"Yeah. If we had a roof, they couldn't pitch snowballs at us over the walls. They couldn't hit us."

"A roof?"

"Sure, Mike. We could hide inside then, and nobody would even know we were there. We could go deep inside and hide and nobody would ever find us. Nobody could hurt us." There was a certain urgency in his voice.

"I don't know how to make a roof," I said.

"We could do it," Ricky said. "We could get boards and lay them across the top and then put snow on them. That would work."

"Maybe," I said. I didn't want to dash his hopes, he was so intent on this idea of a roof.

"Look, Mike. We could lay boards like this." He pointed from wall to wall in the room where he stood. "Then we could cover them up with snow. Then we could go over there," he said and pointed at a passageway, "and put more boards down and cover them up. We could just do that until the whole fort had a roof."

"We could try," I said, "but if we put a roof on it we won't be able to stand up in it."

Ricky considered this for a moment, biting on the tip of his soggy mitten as he thought. "I know what! We could leave the front part like it is and just put a roof on toward the back. It could be our secret part of the fort. We could hide in there if we had to. We could crawl into the secret part."

"Yeah," I said, beginning to see some merit in the plan. "But where are we going to get boards?"

Ricky began to chew on his mitten again, deep in thought. He looked around the yard, his mitten still clenched between his teeth. "I bet there's lots of boards in the alley. I bet we can get boards from behind Nile's or maybe down by Albinson's."

"Maybe," I said.

"Sure," Ricky said. "I bet we can find all the boards we need." "Listen, I think I hear my mom."

We both fell silent, the enchantment of our plans disturbed for the moment.

"*Mi*-chael, time for lunch!" was carried on a cool breeze.

"Come on," I said, "maybe you can have lunch with me and then we can go look for boards."

The two of us raced toward the front of the building, rounding the corner as my mother called out again.

"*Mi*-chael!"

I saw my mother standing on the top step of the main entrance to our building, her arms wrapped tightly about herself to ward off the winter chill that penetrated her thin housedress.

I was about to call out to her when I saw Ricky's mother approaching from the other direction. She was pointing at my mother, as if she were scolding her. At first, I couldn't hear what she was saying, but she obviously had my mother's full attention. Ricky and I slowed to a walk as we neared the two women.

"Oh, no! Oh, no!" Mrs. Stedman said. "The Lord will not abide such behavior. The Lord Jesus does not look kindly on mothers who treat their children so badly." Ricky's mother stood at the bottom of the stone steps, directly in front of my mother. She poked at the air with her finger, her gray eyes narrowed to angry slits. "It pains the Lord to witness sinful things—to see women treat their own flesh and blood so terribly."

My mother stood still, her mouth slack, her eyes wide and frightened and uncomprehending.

"Pray the Lord doesn't strike you dead! You'd better pray to Jesus for forgiveness. Yes, pray for forgiveness, and may the Lord have mercy on you."

I heard a pathetic whimper from Ricky, then he broke and ran to his mother's side. He threw his arms around her waist. "Let's go, Ma. Come on, let's go home," he said as he tugged at her.

Ricky's mother appeared to be completely unaware of her son's presence. "Pray for your soul," she said. And then she abruptly ceased her tirade. She looked down at Ricky, took hold of his hand, and turned and walked away.

Fifteen

My memory of the night Leo came to our home is very selective. Perhaps it is always that way during a time of personal crisis; the mind focuses on some tiny, inconsequential matter in an ugly onslaught of reality. And so what I recall most vividly is how uncomfortable Leo appeared as he stood in the doorway to our apartment.

"My name is Leo Teske, Mrs. Dougherty. I own the ice house just across the alley." He stood there in his khaki pants, overshoes, and navy blue jacket, his hands folded in a way that looked as if he were holding a hat in front of himself. But he had no hat, only the posture of a man displaying deep respect and a timid demeanor.

"Yes?" Mom said as she held the door open.

"I know your boys—and fine boys they are, too, Mrs. Dougherty. You have a beautiful family, if you don't mind me saying so."

Ron and I came into Leo's sight.

"Hello, Ron. Hello, Mike," he said and gave a little finger-wiggling wave, abandoning for a moment his hat-holding posture.

"Hiya," Ron said.

I waved back.

Leo turned back to my mother. "I'm sorry to disturb you, but there was some trouble over at the bar tonight—over at Nile's."

"Please come in, Mr. Teske," Mom said, moving back. She appeared more nervous than Leo when she heard the words *trouble* and *bar*.

Leo stepped into our home, still clutching his imaginary hat. My mother ignored the melted snow that slid in tiny chunks from his overshoes onto our floor. "I just thought someone should let you know."

"What's happened?" Mom asked warily. "Is Pat all right?"

"I'm sure he'll be fine, Mrs. Dougherty."

"Please come in," my mother repeated, and motioned Leo toward the kitchen.

Ron and I followed them. Leo sat down while the three of us stood and listened closely to what he had to say. As he spoke, I watched his big, rough hands. They apparently had become a problem for him—cumbersome appendages that served no useful purpose and had no proper place or way of being set aside. He folded them in his lap, then placed them on the table, then crossed his arms and tucked them under his biceps. He held this position for a while and then laid each of them on his thighs. He rubbed his thighs hard, then tucked his hands under his crossed arms again. "Well, I don't know all of it," he said.

Mom suppressed her anxiety for the moment. "Mr. Teske, would you like a cup of coffee?"

"Oh, no. No, thanks, Mrs. Dougherty." He began to rub his thighs again. "I just—I wanted to let you know what happened, and help if I can. Seems Mr. Dougherty stopped in at Nile's after work. He was all riled up about something, I don't know what. Anyway, he got into an argument with a couple of fellas in the bar. You know how it is when folks have been drinking. They do things they wouldn't normally do."

"Yes," Mom said, hurrying him along.

Leo placed his hands flat on the table, fingers spread wide. "Ah, did you want the boys to hear this?" he said, his voice confidential.

"The boys can stay. Please go on."

Leo crossed his arms, hiding his hands again. "Well, one thing led to another and a fight started. Guess it was pretty rough stuff. Two of these fellas and your husband."

"Oh, my God, where is he now?"

"I'm sure he's okay. I mean, I know he got bruised up some, but the police were called and they broke it up before anyone got hurt real bad."

"Oh, my God," Mom repeated and put a hand to her mouth.

"It's not so bad as it might be," Leo said. "I mean, these cops are pretty decent fellas. I understand they didn't arrest anyone. They just broke it up and took Mr. Dougherty over to General Hospital to get patched up."

I don't recall exactly what images had begun to form in my mind at that moment, or what terrible dread seized me, but I began to cry. They were not tears of great breath-catching sobs, but silent tears of a deep ache of abandonment and sorrow.

"Don't cry," Ron said angrily. "He's okay."

Leo turned and tousled my hair. "Your brother's right, Mike. Your dad is gonna be fine."

I wiped away my tears, embarrassed by my uncontrolled emotion. "I know," I said.

As Leo offered more assurance, the phone rang in the next

room. Mom rushed to answer it, and Leo lowered his words of comfort to a whisper.

"Don't you worry, your daddy is just fine," he said in a hushed voice.

"Yes, this is Mrs. Patrick Dougherty," I heard my mother say into the phone.

"That's probably your dad right now," Leo whispered.

"I understand," Mom said.

"I didn't mean to frighten you boys," Leo whispered to me. "Sometimes these things happen. I've seen lots worse."

"Is he being released now? May I speak to him?"

"See," Leo said. "I bet your dad's coming home right now."

"I see. Yes, I think I can," Mom said. "Yes, I'll be there as soon as I can." Her voice was steady.

"There, you see? Everything is okay," Leo whispered and patted me on the shoulder.

Mom hung up the phone, then picked it up again and dialed. She was talking with someone and making notes on a small pad near the phone. I didn't listen to what she said, or what Leo was saying to me. I only thought about how much I wished none of this had happened, and how much I wished my father didn't drink.

My mother came back to the kitchen. I had never seen her appear so strong and resolute. She displayed no fury, as she had the night she discovered Dad had taken Ron's route money. She wasn't fearful as so often happened when my father's temper flared, nor did she seem particularly sad. She simply spoke in a matter-of-fact manner, advising Ron and me of what we had to do. She was in charge, tapping into some previously hidden source of strength as she took command. "Your father is being released from the hospital, but I need to meet him there. Ron, I want you to go with me."

"Sure, Mom," Ron said.

"If you need a ride, I'd be happy to take you there," Leo offered.

"I'd appreciate that very much, Mr. Teske," she said evenly. "Michael, you'll have to stay here with Katy. If you need anything, you can call the O'Neils. This is their number." She handed me a piece of paper. "Mrs. O'Neil said she'd come right down here if you need anything at all."

My mother was already putting on her coat and boots, and Ron followed her example. "You'll be okay, Michael. We shouldn't be gone more than an hour or so. Just read some comics or listen to the radio. But try not to wake Katy. It'll be easier for you if she sleeps."

"Okay, Mom," I said.

"Lock the door when we leave, and don't let anyone in except the O'Neils."

"I won't."

"Give me a kiss."

Leo stood waiting at the door.

"Ron, are you ready?" Mom asked.

"Yes."

For an instant, just a wisp of time that was less than a heartbeat, I saw something in her eyes as she looked down at me. It was a softness, a fragile sentiment of regret and concern and inexpressible sorrow. It was there, and then it was gone, vanquished by the absolute necessity of maintaining control.

"You'll be fine, Michael. You've got to be my little man now."

Sixteen

As it turned out, it wasn't the fight in the bar that inflicted the real damage. It was what had happened before the fight that was the problem. My father had lost his job—fired from the road for drinking. He had been sent home from the depot only to stop at Nile's and vent his wrath on two strangers. There had been no arrests, and the physical beating he suffered resulted only in a left eye that was discolored and swollen shut, and an L-shaped cut in the center of his lower lip.

I believe he was greatly ashamed of it all—the physical signs of the brawl as well as the humiliation of having lost his job. Over the next several weeks he seldom strayed from the apartment and settled into an unusual silence. It was not the typical brooding, deceptive quiet that could be shattered at any moment, but the shameful resignation of someone who has met with great defeat. Much of the day he would wander from room to room and sigh, stopping to read and reread the paper as he hunched over a cup of coffee in the kitchen and smoked countless cigarettes. In the evening he would listen to Walter Winchell on the radio, grunting at news commentary with which he agreed or disagreed—it was impossible to tell which.

In an odd way, it was not an unpleasant period. Though there was an all-consuming worry about money, my father was not drinking and there was a kind of wounded calm in our lives that was abnormally peaceful. When he and my mother spoke, he assured her that the union would get his job back for him. At first, he said this to her in a way that sounded more apologetic than confident, but as the days went by he professed an unshakable belief that he would, in fact, regain his position on the road. It seemed that he gathered strength from his own words, turning them into truth by simple repetition.

My mother, on the other hand, said very little. She listened patiently, injecting "I hope you're right" and "I'm sure the union will do all they can for us" at appropriate points in my father's monologue. There was going to be some kind of hearing, at which the union was to rescue my father from his disgrace. But as the weeks passed and Dad's optimism grew, Mom was less hopeful. She saw the need for action, and the risk of waiting passively for relief. Her uneasiness with the situation came out fully one night after dinner.

"Pat," she said, fingering the rim of her coffee cup, her eyes cast down at the table, "your hearing has been delayed twice now and I don't think we can wait any longer."

My father leaned back, held his head at a jaunty angle and lit a cigarette. "What do you mean?" he said, squinting one eye in response to the smoke. "What do you mean?" he repeated as he waved out the match and tossed it in the ashtray.

Mom didn't look up. "We've got to have money coming in. The rent is due soon, and I don't think we can sit and wait any longer."

"Look, I'll be back to work in a couple of weeks. Nobody's going to throw us out if the rent is a little late." He rose from his chair and walked to the stove. "You want some more of this?" he said as he began to fill his cup with fresh coffee.

"No thanks."

"I'll tell you something," he said as he poured, "none of this would have happened if it weren't for that goddamn Tobias." The reference was to the railroad official who had stopped my father before he boarded the train, finding him unfit for duty and sending him home. "He's a real bastard."

"Please, Pat, watch your language in front of the boys."

"Well, I mean it," he said. "I've seen plenty of the men show up in a lot worse condition than I was in. I'm telling you, Tobias has it in for me and the union is going to prove it. If they think they can fire every man who's had a beer or two before work, they'll have to can half the railroad."

Mom sighed, touched her hair, and sat up a little straighter as my dad returned to the table. She waited a while before she spoke, and when she did speak, it was with a steady, even voice, without rancor or accusation. "Tobias isn't the problem, Pat. You know that and so do I."

I tensed, expecting my father to fly into a rage. The short silence was unbearable, waiting for the lightning crack of his temper. But it didn't come. Instead, he lowered his head and brushed imaginary crumbs from the tabletop. He spoke as he brushed at the cloth. "So now you're taking their side."

"No," Mom said. She reached across the table and laid her hand on top of his. "I'm not taking anyone's side but yours. But none of this would have happened if you hadn't been drinking." She continued before Dad could object. "Suppose Tobias does have it in for you. I mean, maybe he does. But if that's the case, then it's all the more reason not to drink. Don't give him the chance to hurt you."

Dad pulled his hand away. Mom had gone too far in her candid appraisal. "Jesus Christ, now I don't even have the right to have a goddamn beer!"

"I'm not saying that, Pat. Of course you have a right to have a beer. I'm just saying that drinking before you go to work—especially if this Tobias is against you—it just isn't the thing to do."

This seemed to appease Dad, at least for the moment. To keep peace, she had joined him in his duplicity.

"Well, maybe that's true, damn it. But it isn't right." He picked up his cigarette and took a long drag, exhaling the smoke out his nose and mouth simultaneously. "I'm telling you, though, the union's going to hang his ass on this thing. I've seen them take on these stuffed shirts before, and believe me, they take them to task for the kind of crap they try to pull. I can't wait for that hearing."

"I'm sure you're right, Pat. But as I was saying, we need money right now. I'm sure this thing will get straightened out by the union, but in the meantime the rent still has to be paid and the bills keep coming in."

My father appeared to deflate somewhat, his bravado again confronted by reality. "Listen, I've got plenty of friends. There are guys on that road who'd give me the shirt off their back. And they know I've gotten a raw deal on this thing. Hell, they tried to can Anderson, remember? That was Tobias, too, and he didn't get away with it. No sir, the union stuffed that one right down his throat. If worse comes to worst, there's plenty of them that would be happy to loan me some money till I'm back on my feet."

Mom reached out for Dad's hand again, but he picked his cigarette up from the ashtray and took another drag, leaving her to touch nothing. "I know you don't want that, Pat. You're a proud man, and I know how much it would hurt you to go asking for help."

He didn't respond, except to exhale long streams of smoke from his nostrils.

"But there's something I could do—and should do as your wife. I was talking to Sally Faber, the woman up on third floor who works at the Chef Cafe on Franklin. Sally says there are waitress openings right now and you can just about work any hours you want."

"Jesus Christ! Now my wife wants to go to work. That's just great. You talk about my pride. How proud can I be if I have to send my wife out to work?"

"It's better than borrowing from your friends, and it would just be until you get back on the road. Sally said she brings home five or ten dollars in tips some nights. We could use that kind of money."

"Oh, who the hell listens to Sally. Everybody in the building knows her husband is nothing but a bum, sitting on his ass all day and complaining about his bad back. She's a joke."

"That's not true, Pat." Mom spoke coolly, not pleading with Dad, not cowering before his anger. "It makes sense, Pat. We need some money, and it would be a way to get a little cash immediately. There's no shame in my working to help out until you're back on the road."

My father considered. He leaned forward and stubbed out his cigarette, mashing it hard into the ashtray. "And just who is going to take care of the little one while you're out at work?"

"I could work evenings. I'd be here during the day with Katy. I could have dinner ready for everyone before I left for work. The boys could do the dishes and they'd be here at night to take care of her if she needed anything. Besides, the big tips are at night, so it's really the best time to work anyway. Sally said so."

My father shook his head. "Sally!" he snorted.

"I might as well be helping out, Pat. I could be bringing some money home, instead of doing nothing in the evening," she said, acting as if her nights were filled with leisure—a sop to his delicate sense of pride.

"Well, what do you two boys think of your mother going to work?"

Ron looked directly at Dad. "Fine with me."

"Sure," I said. "I don't care."

My father made an expansive gesture with his arms. "Well, hell, I guess it's all settled then. My wife's going to support the family."

"Pat, please. You know that isn't it at all," Mom said.

"Fine," he said. "That's fine. But, when I get back to work, the waitress crap ends. I won't have people thinking my wife is supporting me. Do you understand?"

"Yes."

Seventeen

I lied when I said I didn't care if my mother went to work. I only said it because I knew that was what she hoped I would say, and because I knew the money was important. She got the job and the evening hours she wanted. It went well for her, and for all of us, I suppose. In the mornings after she had worked, and before Ron and I went off to school, we would help her count the tip money from the previous night. After breakfast, the three of us would make dollar stacks of the nickels and dimes and quarters on the kitchen table. I think her having us help count the tips was a way of making us feel we were part of her effort. She was proud of the money she made for the family, and of being a good waitress. In fact, there were times when I felt that the expressions of appreciation for her work were more of a reward to her than anything else. "My manager told me I'm the best new waitress they have," she'd say as we made little pick up piles of change. "She said customers actually ask to be seated in my station."

I don't think there was ever a morning that we counted out less than five dollars in tips. And more than once the stacks of silver totaled to more than twelve dollars.

But the nights without her lacked warmth. When she was gone, Ron and I stayed indoors after dinner, to do our homework and be available in case Katy needed anything. My father was only a shadowy presence in the house. Except to ask if we had finished our homework or to tell us to see what Katy wanted, he spent most of the night listening to the radio or resting. I know that he came to realize how important it was that she was working, even if he didn't say it. I know too that he missed her. In his oblique, contradictory way, he finally expressed it one night while Ron and I were busy with homework in the kitchen. He came and hovered over us silently, as if he wanted to tell us something but couldn't find the right words. "Kind of quiet around here without your mom, isn't it?" he said at last. "Goddamn railroad!" he added gruffly and left the kitchen. That was as close as he came, but I knew what he meant.

Some nights Ricky came over after dinner, but he could never stay very long and was shier than ever since the day Mrs. Stedman had delivered her strange verbal assault on my mother. One evening, just before he left, he whispered something to me.

"What?" I whispered back.

"Did your mom say anything about my mom? I mean, you know, about the day we were building our fort?"

"Naw," I said. "She didn't say anything. She doesn't care about that stuff." What I told him was mostly true. She *hadn't* said anything directly. She told me that Ricky was welcome in our house anytime, but she preferred that I stay away from the Stedmans' place as much as possible. He was better after our brief exchange, content that nothing had happened to spoil our friendship or jeopardize his acceptance in our home.

There was improvement in my father's life, too. As he had so often predicted, the union was able to return him to work. However, after the repeated delays of his hearing, it was nearly three months from the time he had been dismissed until he was able to get back on the road. Perhaps it was his prolonged unemployment or his prolonged sobriety, or both; but whatever the reason, he did not follow through on his ultimatum that my mother would have to quit waitressing when he returned to work. The topic simply didn't arise, and Mom was clearly pleased to keep her job.

During those three months of my father's inactivity, both Ron's birthday and mine came and went—mine in January and Ron's in February. Because my Mom was working, we were each able to receive gifts and have a small celebration. There were cards and money from Grandma Dougherty and Aunt Marie, and new buckle galoshes for me from my parents, and a blue wool sweater for Ron. We each had a special cake and our choice of dinners. Ricky was invited to both parties, and came to each one with a card and fifty cents. All the money I received—three dollars and fifty cents—I confided to Ricky would be spent on caps in the spring. He flashed a conspiratorial grin at hearing my good news.

The school year dragged on into the lengthening days of March. The early spring winds warmed, turning from north to west, melting the snowcover and revealing great patches of earth. Then, winter struggled against the inevitable, conjuring up a storm that coated the ground once again with heavy, wet snow that lasted a day or two and melted away. Snow for slush balls and icy shocks that were dropped down the backs of unsuspecting students as they walked home from school.

"I'm gonna get that Bojelski," I said to Ricky as I pulled the back of my shirt out of my pants and swiped awkwardly at chunks of wet ice that slid down my spine and gathered at my belt line. "Look up by my collar, Ricky. Is there anymore around my neck?"

"Nope."

"I'm gonna get that Bojelski!"

"Yeah. He sure can run fast though."

"Not fast enough. I'll get him tomorrow. You'll see."

Ricky nodded and fell in step beside me as I tucked my shirt back in my pants. "This stuff might not even last till tomorrow," he said.

"I don't care. I'm gonna get him anyway."

"Yeah," Ricky said as he broke into a kind of shuffling half-skip, kicking his left foot forward, then drawing up the right, then repeating the movement again and again. "Won't be long till spring."

"Yeah," I said, my hostility evaporating along with the snow. "Miss Tremble said she's going to take our class on a picnic when the weather gets nice—before summer vacation."

"Yeah?"

"Yeah. Maybe I'll get Bojelski then."

Ricky reverted to a normal gait. "Maybe," he said. "Or maybe you guys will be friends by then."

"I doubt it," I said.

Ricky lowered his head, his mood more serious. "I hope we'll always be friends."

"Sure we will be," I said quickly. "Why wouldn't we be?" It was one of those odd Ricky-questions.

"I don't know. Stuff changes. I just hope we're always friends." He raised his head and smiled, his face bright and idea-shiny. "You know what we ought to do? We ought to make one of those—what do you call it—one of those promises. No matter what happens, we'll promise to meet when we're lots older—like twenty years old. What do you call that?"

"What?"

"A promise you have to keep? You know, a special promise that you keep for years and years and never forget. What do you call that?"

"A pact, I think."

"Yeah," Ricky said, "that's it—a pact." In his excitement he stopped walking and grabbed hold of me by the shoulders. "We'll make a pact. No matter what happens—if either one of us moves or gets married or whatever happens—we'll meet when we're twenty years old. We'll meet on the first of July the summer we're both twenty. What do you say?"

"Sure," I said automatically.

"No, really, Mike. I mean it. We'll meet on the first of July when we're twenty."

"Okay," I said more thoughtfully. "Where will we meet?"

For a moment he was absolutely motionless, except for his eyes. They searched skyward for an answer—and found it. "Rotograph's, where I first met you and Ron. Remember?"

"Sure, I remember."

"You can bring Ron, too. The three of us will meet at Rotograph's. Okay?"

"Sure," I said.

"We have to shake on it." He held out his hand and I shook it. "A pact!" he declared formally as he shook my hand. "No matter what happens," he said in a way that left no doubt I was to answer in kind.

"No matter what happens," I said.

Eighteen

The tenuous peace that had settled on our home early that spring was broken, as so many quiet periods had been shattered before. In a single night, the bright, elusive promise of stability was gone.

Ron and Katy and I were in bed for the night, supposedly asleep. But I couldn't sleep, aware that my father was sitting alone in the kitchen waiting for my mother to come home from work. Waiting and drinking from a pint bottle of whiskey. He had been drinking even before he came home, before he opened the fresh bottle that sat before him on the table. His anger was reflected in the fact that it was the first time he ever openly drank in front of us. He made no attempt to conceal his behavior, and Ron and I responded to this by silently hurrying through our chores and our homework and avoiding him as we prepared for bed.

I knew something was wrong, and I couldn't relax as I listened to the *clink* of his drinking glass as he set it on the table again and again. I could hear the *scratch-flare* of the match as he lit each cigarette. From the couch, deep into the night, I thought I could even hear his breathing—deep and full. It must have been nearly midnight when I heard the door to our apartment open and the hushed sounds of my mother's return.

"Pat!" she said in a whisper. "You're still up."

"So it seems."

"Is everything all right? Are the children okay?"

"They've been asleep for hours."

I could hear my mother moving about, removing her coat and shoes. She must have spotted the bottle of whiskey. "Pat, you're drinking!"

"Nooo!" my father drawled.

"Oh, Pat, why?"

"Why not?"

She said nothing, obviously trying to avoid his lurking hostility.

"I thought I'd just relax and have a few drinks while my wife was out making lots of tips!" He emphasized and spat out the last word. "Did you make lots of tips tonight?"

"Yes, we were busy. I think we got the entire crowd from the Franklin Theater."

"You and the boys count that money every morning, don't you? You sit around and count it and talk about it, don't you?" They were more accusations than questions.

"Yes, we do."

"You do! You tell the boys how you make all those tips?"

My mother exhaled slowly. "Pat, I'm tired. I've been on my feet all evening. What is this all about?"

"Why, hell, it isn't about anything. What would it be about? I'm just sitting here having a few drinks to toast my wife—the goddamn princess of the Chef Cafe."

I heard my mother leave the kitchen and walk toward the bedroom. "You're drunk, Pat. I won't talk to you when you're like this."

There was an explosive crack from the kitchen—the sound of my father's chair as it was hurled backward against the wall. "You goddamn better talk to me. You get your ass back in here this minute!" he shouted.

"Oh God, Pat, stop. You'll wake the children."

"I don't give a good goddamn if I wake the whole neighborhood. You get your ass back in here!"

I heard my mother walking back to the kitchen. For a moment, I couldn't breathe, as if all the air had vanished from the room. I raised my hands to cover my ears, and then my mouth to muffle any sounds of torment that might escape.

"Pat, I don't know what this is all about, but I think it would be best if we waited to discuss it until morning."

I heard my father push his chair back up to the table. "Well, I don't think it'll keep till morning. How the hell do you like *that?*" he shouted.

"All right, fine. Just tell me what this is all about, and please lower your voice."

"You don't know Johnny Larson, do you?" There was a sneer in his voice.

"No, I don't. I've heard you mention him, but I've never met the man."

"Well, he knows you. He had dinner a couple of nights ago at the Chef. He saw you working. Saw you swishing your ass all over the restaurant—smiling and flirting and wiggling your little behind all over the place."

"What are you saying, Pat?" Mom's voice shook with indignation, and she sounded like she was going to cry.

"He said you were flirting with every guy in the place. Tip

money! Tips for what?"

"You bastard! I won't listen to another word of this. Tell your filthy-minded friend to go to hell."

"No, goddamn it, I'll tell you what you're gonna do. You're gonna quit that goddamn job and act like a wife and mother again."

"I'm not going to quit my job!" she shouted at him, matching his fury.

"The hell you aren't," he growled. "You think you're pretty cute since you went to work. You think you can have everything your own way. Well, I'm still the head of this house and I'm telling you you're quitting that job."

Strangely, the shouting was broken by the sound of laughter. My mother was laughing—long, rolling, mirthless laughter. Laughter that stopped and started again, and ended in tears. "Oh yes," she said at last, "I think I can have everything my way." She began to laugh again. "Yes, Pat, this is how I want things—living in a basement with my three children, wondering every day if maybe this is the day my husband is going to drink himself out of a job. I'm barely able to pay the rent or give the kids decent clothes. And then, when I try to help, when my husband gets fired from the road, when I try to hold things together by going out to work, I get accused of being a whore! That's my idea of paradise, Pat."

"Shut up!"

She was crying now, but not uncontrollably. "Yes, Pat, I'll shut up now. And you know why? Because I just don't give a damn anymore, Pat. I can't take this anymore. I don't want to fight with you, but I'm not quitting my job. You can sit here and drink yourself stupid, I'm going to bed now."

"Listen to me, you smart-mouth little bitch. You're going to quit that job or I'll go down there myself and see that they get rid of you."

Mom exploded. "You stay away from there! I've found one little corner of life where I'm valued and treated with respect and can show something for my efforts, and I won't let you ruin it." Now the tears were mixed with consuming rage. "Ruin yourself if that's what you want, but leave something for me."

"You'd better shut that smart mouth of yours, or I'll slap it shut for you!"

The door to the bedroom opened. Ron stepped into the living room, his face puffy with sleep. He rubbed his eyes and stared at me until he was sure I was awake. "What's going on?" he said.

"Mom and Dad are fighting."

"What about?"

"Her job. He's really drunk and—"

"Listen," he said, and held his hand up to silence me.

They were fighting now about why my father had given up his work as a musician. Everything in his life—everything meaningful—had been sacrificed for her, and for us.

"Lies, Pat! They're all lies, and you know it. The only thing you've ever really cared about is yourself and your booze. You wouldn't give a damn if the kids and I starved to death, as long as you could get your hands on a drink!"

"Shut that goddamn mouth," he roared, "or I swear to God I'll shut it for you!"

The shouting stopped. There was a sickening rumble of furniture, then a high-pitched scream and an explosion of breaking glass. Ron bolted toward the kitchen. I jumped up from the couch and chased after him.

Behind me, from the bedroom, I could hear Katy crying. Just in front of me, in the yellow glow of the kitchen, I saw Ron charge toward our parents. "Leave her alone," he screamed and hurled himself at Dad. He struck him, waist-level, and they both crashed up against the wall.

"What the hell do you think you're doing, you little snot!"

Ron's face was flushed and teary. "Leave her alone! I hate you!"

"Get the hell away from me," Dad said. He shoved Ron in the chest, hard. The single motion sent Ron sprawling backward. He fell to the floor, both hands landing flat on the surface amid shards of the broken glass. Ron screamed and lifted both hands from the floor immediately, as if they had come in contact with a white-hot stove. They were already covered with blood.

Mom ran to Ron, grasped his hands, and turned them, palms up, for examination. "Michael, go get the Band-Aid box and Mercurochrome. Hurry!"

Ron ignored his wounds as Mom led him to the kitchen sink. He glared at Dad, his face still crimson. "I hate you!"

"I didn't mean to hurt the boy," Dad sounded more sober and faintly contrite. "I just reacted. I just gave him a lousy little shove."

Mom ignored him as she ran water over Ron's cuts, picking glass out of his hands and dabbing at them with sterile gauze. Then she took the Mercurochrome from me. "Just stay away from us," she said without looking up from her task. "Just please stay away from us. I think you've done enough for one night."

"Fine. You don't want me around, I'm going out." He left the kitchen, grabbed a jacket from the closet, and slammed the apartment door as he left.

Nineteen

Sobriety followed Ron's injuries, but this time there was no evidence of forgiveness on Mom's part. My parents spoke only when they couldn't avoid it, to simply get through the daily necessities. There was no hint of tenderness or caring or mutual pleasure in even the tiniest joys of life. They were strangers, sharing only a common space that was filled with resentment and mistrust and increasing bitterness. The great bulwark of my mother's love was finally eroding from the repeated assaults on her spirit. Her love, once so fiercely loyal and unshakable, was no longer beyond question.

She kept her job, as she said she would. There was no further discussion or argument about it, though I'm sure it remained a flashpoint for both of them, just beneath the superficial calm. The three of us still counted tips each morning after my mother had worked, though it was less of a celebration now—marred by my father's resentments and the scurrilous accusations he had made.

On those nights when Mom was home and Dad was on the road, there were furtive calls to Aunt Marie. I could hear her on the phone late at night when we were all supposed to be asleep. I couldn't hear all of the conversation, just bits and pieces, but enough to realize Mom wanted a change. Or maybe it was just that she needed to tell someone about her life, and comfort herself by giving voice to her thoughts of escape. Whatever it was, the calls were important to her, I'm sure. They must at least have served as a lifeline of possibilities, allowing her to survive each day. There was talk of separation and taking us three children to live with Aunt Marie in Alexandria. There was talk of calling the police if she or any of us were ever harmed again, no matter how unintentional the injury, if it came about because of his drinking. More hopefully, there were thoughts of seeing the parish priest to seek guidance in their troubled marriage. And once, there was talk of commitment proceedings. I listened to the calls, garnering as much information as I could, lulling myself to sleep with vague hopes and fears of some dramatic change in our existence.

But there was no real change, except for the coming of spring. While the process had been gradual, the realization was sudden. In a single night, our avenue had become green and pastoral, the branches of the elm trees reaching out to each other, spanning the width of the street and creating a canopy of green lace. The world had transformed itself from shades of cold slate gray and white to a place of warmth and color. The wind no longer swept through barren branches unabated, but created a gentle rustling sound in the newly leafed trees.

Ricky and I discovered spring together one day after school, prolonging our walk home in the brilliant sunshine. Though we both knew we'd be in trouble for not coming home directly, we said nothing about it to each other and casually agreed to split a suicide Coke at Rotograph's. When we were done, we left the drugstore and headed toward Elliot, just beyond the ice house and the alley.

Leo sat in front of the ice house, his chair tipped back against the shack, a neighborhood symbol that the season had changed. "Hello, boys," he called out to us, ever vigilant despite his slumberous appearance.

"Hiya," I called back.

Ricky waved.

"How's the family?" Leo said as he sat forward and brought his chair to rest on the ground.

"Everybody's fine," I said. I didn't mind his questions anymore. Since the night he had helped us, I had come to see him in a different light. I didn't know exactly what to think of him, but I felt he could be trusted.

"That's good to hear. That's good to hear," he repeated.

"Yeah," I said. "And how are you, sir?" I had never thought to ask him that before.

Leo smiled so broadly that his eyes disappeared. He lowered his head and nodded several times. When he looked up, his eyes glistened in the spring sun like dark, tiny crystals before a flame. "I'm just fine. Couldn't be better."

"Good," I said. I waited for more questions, but Leo just started nodding his head again. "Well, see ya," I said as Ricky and I walked away.

"So long, boys, and thanks for asking after me, Michael."

I just waved without looking back.

"He's okay," Ricky said, his intonation causing the words to hover between a statement of fact and a question.

"Leo's a good guy. He helped us one night when there was some trouble."

"Oh."

"Sometimes . . ." I hesitated. "One night my dad had too much to drink and there was some trouble. Anyway, old Leo helped us." I couldn't tell it all. Some things were not discussed outside the family—not even with your closest friend.

We walked along in silence, and I immediately wished I hadn't said anything about my father's drinking. I could talk to Ricky about anything—except that. That was understood.

"Do you ever pray?" Ricky said at last.

It was a totally unrelated question, but I was relieved that he had changed the subject. "Sure," I said. "Me and Ron go to church almost every Sunday with the O'Neils."

"No, I don't mean in church," he said intently. "Do you pray at home?"

"Sometimes," I said. "My mom tells us to say our prayers when we go to bed. She works nights a lot now, so she isn't always there to remind us, but I know she wants us to pray."

Ricky's face contorted in frustration, the little blue eyes becoming slits of disappointment with my failure to understand what he was trying to ask. "I mean, does your mom or dad pray with you? Do they make you pray until you say it just right?"

"No, they don't pray with us."

"Never?"

"No, I don't think so."

Ricky stopped and turned toward me. "Then they don't tell you if you're praying wrong?"

"I don't get it. What do you mean praying wrong? You just pray, don't you?"

"Come here," Ricky said. He led me behind our building, into the oversized yard where our great fortress of snow had once stood.

The yard was untouched by the magic of spring. Hidden in shadow most of the day, it was a great, dark, grassless expanse, rich with the smell of moist, black earth. It was an ideal place to reveal the most secret corners of your life.

When we were deep into the yard, Ricky stopped. He looked

directly into my eyes. His face was hard and unflinching, but his voice just above a whisper. "We have to make another pact."

"Okay. What about?"

"You can't ever tell anybody what I'm going to tell you."

"Okay."

"No matter what happens."

"Right," I said.

"My mom," he began his most intimate revelation, "makes me pray almost every night." He spoke in a monotone, as if what he was about to tell me could only be said in a voice lacking in all emotion, or it couldn't be said at all. "But I always get it wrong."

"You mean the words? I learned lots of prayers for my first communion. I could teach you the words."

"No, not the words," he said in his low monotone voice. "It's something else. Something about being unworthy. I don't know exactly, except I almost always get it wrong. And when I get it wrong . . . When it's wrong, I have to be hit."

"What do you mean?"

Ricky turned around, his back to me. "Here," he said as he pulled his green-and-orange-striped T-shirt out of his jeans. "Pull up my shirt,"

I did as he asked.

"Higher," he said. He repeated his instruction until his fragile shoulder blades, looking like white, undeveloped wings, were fully exposed. "Can you see?"

Splayed across the top of his back, V-shaped, were linear scars of purple and white. The raised lines stretched from either side of the knobs of his spine and angled upward across the tiny ridges of skin that looked so much like infant wings. The ugly, discolored welts of flesh that had been broken and healed and broken again bore silent witness to his constant state of unworthiness. "Yeah," I said, trying to keep my voice from betraying shock. "I can see."

Ricky pulled his shirt down and turned back to me. "It's bad, Mike, 'cause no matter how much I pray or how hard I try, I can't seem to ever get it right."

"Your mom shouldn't do that. She shouldn't hit you. My mom or the O'Neils would never do that."

"Never?"

"Never. I mean, not 'cause of the way we say prayers. Maybe, if I did something really bad, my mom might give me a swat on my butt or something, but my parents would . . ." I thought of Ron, and the night his hands were cut so badly. It was a secret that couldn't be hinted at outside the family. "Anyway," I began again, "I think it's really weird to get hit for saying prayers wrong." I couldn't say anything more.

"I know," he said, his voice no longer flat and indifferent. "Sometimes I think about running away, except I don't know where I'd go. At night before I go to sleep, if it's been really bad, I take out my picture of my dad and talk to him. I think about the two of us just going away together somewhere. But, I don't know where we'd go. Probably sounds really stupid to you, right?"

"No. It doesn't sound stupid. I've thought about leaving home sometimes."

"You have?"

"Yeah."

He looked at me and smiled, his blue eyes coming back to life. Curiously, he didn't ask why I might want to leave home, or if he and I might develop some grand scheme together. It was as if all the comfort and solace in the world was his, simply knowing that at times I shared his desire for a different life. He tucked his shirt a little deeper into his jeans and said only that it was way past time for us to be home.

Twenty

I was haunted by the secret Ricky had shared with me, but I kept our pact and told no one. What he had shown me was so ugly and frightening to me that I could barely even talk about it with Ricky, though I thought of it often and wondered if the beatings continued. Sometimes, at night, I imagined hearing him scream as he was struck over and over as punishment for his unworthiness. And I wondered how the God we worshiped with the O'Neils could let this happen. I wanted to ask the O'Neils about that, or maybe even Father Zimmerman, but that would have violated the solemn oath I had taken.

For weeks after Ricky told me about it, when we were alone, I would ask him how things were at home. He would just look at me, smile thinly, and say it wasn't so bad. He never said more than that, and he never showed me the marks again. In time, the knowledge of his beatings was banished to some obscure edge of my consciousness, lost in the swirling excitement of the final days of school and cap gun fights in the lengthening twilight and helping Ron with his paper route—that child's world that stubbornly exists even within the most nightmarish reality adults can create. But, ultimately, Ricky's torment was completely eclipsed by the growing crisis in our own home.

Dad's drinking was getting worse, his periods of sobriety more fleeting. The conflict in our home was nearly constant, devoid of the previous interludes of artificial tranquillity, and expressed more and more in physical violence.

An inch or two above the kitchen sink, the plaster wall displayed a star-shaped chip, made by a plate that Dad had hurled at Mom. There were bruises on her legs and arms, evidence of fights while Ron and I were at school. The bruises evolved to dark purple islands surrounded by a yellowish-green border, only to be replaced by fresh blue welts before they had faded completely. On most days, when we returned from school, she had been crying. And always there was a look in her eyes—not of anger or sorrow or contempt, but of resignation or hopelessness. It was there when she played with Katy, or counted tips, or baked bread, or cleaned the apartment, or smiled bravely at Ron and me and pretended to be happy.

Dad's drinking was no longer hidden, if it ever really had been. Now, there were times during the day when he walked the streets in a stumbling, alcoholic haze. His condition was no longer concealed in our apartment or the dark corners of bars, but paraded in front of the neighborhood—and the O'Neils and Leo and Ricky and anyone who sat on the great stone steps that faced the avenue. Illusions of normality could no longer be sustained, not to others and not to ourselves. Yet, incredibly, through all of this, he somehow managed to keep his job. Some days my mother called the railroad to say he was sick, and some days he risked working when he was less than sober. No doubt he had friends on the road who tried to protect him, but the outcome of his deterioration was inevitable.

My mother made fewer calls to Aunt Marie now, perhaps because she was no longer able to comfort herself with those long-distance fantasies. More and more she turned to Ron for advice and logic, if only to confirm what she knew to be true. Her life was intolerable, set on a destructive path that had to be changed before it consumed us all. She knew it, and sought Ron's support for a decision she must have already made.

Late one evening, while Katy and I sat on the couch and looked at comics, I listened to Mom and Ron in the next room. My inattention frustrated Katy, who slapped me on the shoulder and shrieked that it was time to turn the page when she had finished explaining all the pictures to me. My awareness of her was so remote that only her periodic slaps and the odor of Vicks VapoRub that wafted up from her tiny chest reminded me of her presence.

"And Tubby sticked out his tongue. Right?" A rattling sound in her chest. A distant cough. "Right?" A sigh. *Slap!* "Turn the page, Mike! Turn the page!"

"Sorry," I said. I turned the page and strained to hear the hushed voices.

"I don't know what to do," Mom said.

"You can't live like this anymore," Ron said. "You have to leave him. He's drunk all the time and he hits you. Everybody knows it. He's just getting worse and worse."

"You mean divorce him?"

"Yeah."

"I can't do that, Ron. You know that. It's against our religion—against everything I believe in."

Ron spoke with irrefutable logic. "But you can't keep living this way, you've said it yourself. So, if you won't divorce him and you can't live with him, you have to sign the papers."

I knew that they were talking about commitment proceedings, though my understanding of exactly what that entailed was sketchy at best. I understood that Dad would be taken away from the family and sent to some kind of hospital, but I had no idea where he would go or for what length of time.

"I don't know, Ron. I've heard that once they are placed in a state hospital, sometimes they never come out. What if they say your father is . . ." She cleared her throat and began again. "What if they say he is insane? We might never see him again. I've heard that that can happen. They put people in those places, and they . . . and they . . ." Her voice faded into tears.

From the next room there was only the sound of her crying softly. Perhaps she thought of a time when they were young and in love and so full of fresh, bright expectations. They were the handsome young musician and his beautiful lady, facing life unafraid, confident that they could capture all the sparkling prizes the world offered. It had begun that way, amid the spinning, dazzling ballroom lights. Their lives had been filled with music and dancing and laughter, and their dreams must have seemed as reachable as the reflected stars from a revolving ballroom globe. And it had come to this.

A whiff of Vicks. *Slap!* "Turn the page, Mike. Lulu is kying. See, she's kying."

"Oh, yes. You're right, Lulu is crying." I turned the page and listened.

"I don't know, Mom. I don't know what might happen. But I know you can't keep living with him."

Mom sighed. "Oh, Ron, what can we do? I don't even know if I can support all of us on what I make at the Chef. Even with tips, it would be nearly impossible."

Ron was undaunted. "He drinks up all the money he makes anyway. And he's gonna get fired again. You know he will. You've said it."

"Yes."

"We'll make it somehow," he assured her.

There was another long pause before my mom spoke again. "I still love him, somehow. I know that can't make any sense to you at all, I wouldn't expect it to. But, I still love him—or want to, I don't know. And maybe . . . he might never forgive me for doing something like this."

There was no response from Ron. He had no reference point for the sort of turbulent emotions she struggled to express. There was no room for uncertainty or sentiment in the framework of his thirteen-year-old reasoning. There was only one problem and only one alternative.

The warning smell of Vicks again. I turned the page.

Mom sighed. "He can be so good, so loving. You and Michael don't remember. But, before you were born . . . it was so different then." What she said tugged at a dark corner of fear and guilt in me. Perhaps, somehow, we were to blame. It was my fault, and Ron's, and Katy's.

"He's not that way anymore," Ron said.

"I know." Without seeing her, I knew that she was composing herself—sitting up a little straighter, patting hair that had fallen out of place, wiping away wasted tears. "It won't be easy, Ron. If I do this, in some ways it will be tougher than it's ever been before."

"I know. But he won't be here to hurt you and make you cry. He won't be here to kick you and throw things and scare Mike and Katy. That'll make it lots easier in some ways." He paused, but Mom said nothing. Then, grudgingly he added, "Maybe he'll get better, too."

There was the rustle of clothing and a quick catching of breath. I knew that at that moment Mom was embracing Ron, clinging to her older son and her last, faint hope.

Katy's face loomed in front of me. "Are you kying for Lulu, Mike?"

"No," I said and turned the page.

Twenty-One

"Michael! Michael Dougherty!" It was Leo, away from his usual post in front of the ice house.

Ricky and I stopped, our neighborhood askew and requiring a moment of reorientation. "Hi," I said, recovering from my surprise.

Leo bent forward from the waist, his woolly head nearly level with my own. "Are you heading home?"

"Yeah. Me and Ricky are going to my place."

He put a big paw of a hand on my shoulder. "I'd like to talk with you first, if I could."

"Sure," I said.

"Ah, maybe it would be best if Ricky went on home."

"Why?" I said, feeling a vague sense of dread.

"Well, this is a private, sort of man-to-man thing."

"I don't get it," I said.

Leo straightened, a faraway look in his eyes. He wiped his mouth and chin with his giant hand as he thought. "I know. How about you and Ricky and me walk down to the drugstore.

I'll buy us each a soda, and maybe we can talk there—just the two of us."

"Okay with me," I said. "Okay with you, Ricky?"

"Sure."

Ricky and I walked along together, with Leo close behind. When we got to Rotograph's, Leo directed Ricky to one of the stools at the fountain and told him to order anything he wanted. He took me to one of the round tables and slid one of three black, metal-wire chairs to the side. After he had created our table for two and I had ordered a suicide Coke, Leo stared for a moment at the black-and-white checkerboard tile floor. Finally, he looked up at me and flashed a nervous smile. "Your mom told me where I'd find you."

"Yeah?"

"Yes sir. You see, she wanted me to kind of explain some-thing to you before you got home."

"Something's wrong, isn't it?"

Leo held up his hand, signaling me not to panic. "In a way, yes. But everything's been taken care of, and everybody is okay."

"What happened?"

"Well, I'll tell you. You know how things haven't been too good at home—I mean with your father and all."

I could feel my cheeks grow warm and tears gathering in my eyes, but I didn't want to let Leo see me cry. I turned and looked toward Ricky who sat atop one of the high stools at the foun-tain, his back to me, his legs swinging freely beneath the seat of the stool. I looked beyond him at a calendar hanging next to the mirror that ran the length of the fountain. There was a picture of Babe Ruth on the calendar, his face and shoulders formed among clouds in a brilliant blue sky. The spirit and misty face of the Babe smiled down on a young boy at bat in a sandlot game.

I stared at the painting of the legendary ballplayer who had died the previous August.

I felt Leo touch my shoulder. "Michael," he said, compelling me back to the moment, "there's no reason for you to be upset or feel embarrassed. What a father does ain't the fault of the son. You've got nothing to be ashamed about."

For some reason, what he said only made me feel worse. I looked back at Babe Ruth, his cloudy face blurred by my tears.

"Mike, look at me. You have nothing to feel bad about."

My tears, despite all my effort to control them, broke and spilled down my cheeks. "What happened?" I blurted out.

"I'll tell you—all of it. You see, they took your dad away today, and I don't think you'll see him for a long time. He'll be fine, and there'll be lots of people—doctors and people—to help him. Uh, they'll help him . . ."—he groped for words—"get over all this."

"He was drunk, wasn't he?"

Leo nodded

"Did he hurt anyone? Is my mom okay?"

"Now, that's the thing." He cleared his throat noisily. "She's looking a little rough right now, but there's really no reason to worry."

"What did he do?" I shouted. I jumped up so quickly that my chair toppled backward onto the floor.

Ricky swung around on his stool, a startled look on his face. Leo was already on his feet, picking up my chair, trying to reassure both Ricky and me simultaneously. "Sit down, Mike. Take it easy. Just go ahead and finish your soda, Ricky. Mike's okay."

I sat, offering no resistance to the giant hands that gently guided me by the shoulders. I turned and looked at Babe Ruth's grinning face. "What'd he do?" I said.

"Michael, things are only going to get better now, believe me."

"What did he do?" I persisted.

Leo exhaled a long sigh of discomfort. "All right, no punches pulled, I'll just tell you straight out. You're a big guy and I know you can handle it."

He met my gaze, hesitated a moment, then began. "Your dad got himself all liquored up today, down on Franklin Avenue. He was in a real ornery mood—real ornery. Anyway, he went on over to the Chef Cafe and started some trouble, ranting and raving about your mom working there and how he didn't want her there anymore. The manager and your dad got into a shoving match, him asking your dad to leave and all. Anyway, one thing led to another and your dad sort of fell through the display case—you know, that big glass cabinet where they have the cash register?"

Ricky approached cautiously from my left. "Mike?"

"What?" I said, sniffing back my tears and looking straight ahead at Leo.

"I gotta go. I was supposed to be home by now. If it's okay, I gotta go."

"Sure," I said, not looking at him.

He hovered there for a moment, unsure of himself. "You okay?"

"Yeah, sure." I said it as pleasantly and normally as I could manage. "I'll see ya."

"Okay. I'll see ya." He backed away from the table, then turned and walked to the door. "Thanks for the soda," he called out over his shoulder, and he was gone.

"Anyway," Leo went on, trying not to break his rhythm, now that it was all being told, "your dad didn't even get hurt. All that broken glass and not even a scratch. Well sir, that manager thinks so highly of your mom that he didn't even call the police or anything." Leo reflected. "Maybe that wasn't such a good idea, when you think about it."

"But what about my mom?"

"Well, I guess what happened in the Chef only riled your dad up more. I seen him coming down the street headed for home. I could see he was plenty mad and had been drinking. I said hello to him, but he didn't answer. I knew there was gonna be trouble—I could smell it. So, a couple of minutes after he went by, I made it my business to go on over to your place."

"You went there?" I sniffed.

"Yeah. It sounded pretty bad—lots of hollering and things breaking. So, I banged on the door. Some of your neighbors came out to see what was going on, too. Well, your mom finally opened the door and said for me to help her."

"Was she hurt? Was Katy okay?"

"Katy was fine and your mom wasn't so bad. Her face was all red and she was crying, like maybe he'd been slapping her or something. Mostly, he'd been throwing things, I think. There was lots of stuff broken—pictures, dishes, a chair—it was an awful mess. Anyway, I sort of . . . well, I kept him quiet while one of your neighbors called the police."

I began to cry, deeply and without restraint. Leo waited until my crying trailed off into a series of hiccuping sobs, then he handed me a napkin to wipe my face. "It's 'cause of us," I managed to get out between sobs.

"What?"

"My mom said they were happy, and my dad was okay, before we were born." Two hiccuping breaths. "It's because of me and Ron and Katy."

"That ain't true. Don't ever think that. Never!" he said vehemently. "If your mom said that, it was because she was angry and confused. She couldn't have really meant anything like that. You kids are the brightest part of their lives. I know that for a fact. Don't you ever think that. Don't ever say it. Do you hear me?"

"Yes sir."

Leo was visibly shaken. He muttered something, cleared his throat, and rubbed his hands together nervously. "Now," he finally managed, "your brother and your friends the O'Neils are with your mom and Katy. They're cleaning everything up at home."

I looked again at Babe Ruth. He was still smiling down at the boy at bat—captured forever in the rapturous blue sky, the boy forever awaiting the release of the pitch. "Did my mom commit him?" I asked, still not fully understanding what that meant.

Leo gathered his thoughts. "She's gonna, I'm sure. It's for the best. You have to understand that. He'll be getting lots of help to stop drinking."

"Sure," I said woodenly, no longer able to believe that he would ever change.

"Mike, I don't want you to hate your dad, and don't blame yourself. His drinking was a bad mistake he made. He's just one of those folks that started drinking and then it got the best of him. In a way, it ain't nobody's fault. He just made the mistake of starting, and he couldn't stop. He needs help, and now he'll get it. The things he's done, he only did because he was crazy out of his mind with booze. It's not like it's really him."

"Sure."

"Your mom had to do what she's done, and she did it because she loves him. And she wants you to love him, too, I'm sure of it."

"I know."

Leo looked painfully uncertain of what to do or say next. "You want to finish your Coke?" he said at last.

"No." I pushed the glass away and wiped my face again with the napkin. "I guess maybe I should go home and see my mom now. Maybe I can help her."

"Are you sure you want to go?"

"Yeah, I'm sure."

"Okay then, let me take you home."

We walked side by side to the door, Leo's great hand all warm and heavy and comforting on my back. He held the door open for me and forced a lopsided smile. "It's gonna be okay, Mike. Your dad will get better. Don't hate him for what he's done. I know it's hard to understand, but I think deep down he really don't mean harm to no one."

—

When I got home, the O'Neils were still there, consoling my mother and cleaning up the debris from my father's rampage. Mrs. O'Neil was rubbing Mom's back, moving her right hand in slow circles and whispering words of kindness and support while her husband swept broken glass and porcelain into a brown paper bag. When Leo and I stepped through the door, I ran to my Mom's open arms and hugged her as tight as I could, holding on to the lonely pillar of our family.

She held me close and spoke to Leo. "Thank you, Mr. Teske. Thank you for everything."

"You're very welcome, Mrs. Dougherty. I was glad to be of help. If there's anything I can do, you just let me know. I'll be going now."

We still held each other close as she said, "You don't need to hurry off. Would you like to stay and have some coffee?"

Leo's voice grew smaller, and I could hear him pulling the door shut after himself. "Thank you, no. I've really got to get back to work now."

Still my mother and I held on tight. "Did Mr. Teske tell you your father is gone?"

I looked up at her and nodded. I could see that the left side of her face was red and swollen. It was too painful to see and I looked away.

My awareness of our surroundings began to expand, to gather in the rest of the room. The O'Neils and Ron had cleaned up the worst of it, but the destruction was still evident. Here and there, bits of shattered plates still littered the floor, broken drawers sat atop the cupboard, and a chair with only three legs leaned against a corner of the room. It looked like a tornado had been unleashed inside our apartment.

Ron approached, his hands cupped as if he were holding a dying sparrow. "Look what I found, Mom."

He handed her the postcard of the Monet painting. She released me and took the card, holding it with both hands, studying it with sorrow and disbelief. It was torn in the center, and beneath the Monet sky, the women with parasols were scratched and covered with grit. The beauty of that summer day was marred forever.

"Oh no," she said weakly and began to cry. "It must have fallen out of one of the drawers." She wiped her face. "We'll keep it anyway," she said with resolve.

Twenty-Two

My father was sent to the state hospital in Willmar, a small town ninety miles west of Minneapolis. He was to be held there for a period of three months. And despite all the anticipation, the change that resulted from his absence was more profound than I could have imagined.

Life was no longer a matter of fear. A light left on in a room was simply a light left on in a room, not cause for wild ravings. If Katy fell and cried, it was only reason to offer aid and assure her that she was all right. Dinners were peaceful gatherings at which we could all speak freely, without concern about our choice of words and the sensitivity of a subject. Conversations did not need to be carried on in hushed tones, and there was no need for furtive phone calls or lies about what happened in our home.

Most of the time, I didn't think about Dad at all. I simply reveled in the warmth and stability of our lives, without thinking about his eventual return. But there were moments when my mind turned to what had happened and what was yet to come. And there were dreams of destructive rage that clawed at me.

Sometimes the dreams awakened me and made me realize that I wished Dad would never come back.

We could go on peaceably without him. The train rides and singular expressions of affection were too rare and too remote to create any desire for his presence. My most vivid memories were of drunken brawls and broken dishes and insults and tears. I didn't believe that any of it could ever change with him there, and I wanted never again to experience life with him. There had been too much pain and too many disappointments. And finally, in the darkest, most shameful corner of my heart, I wished that he would cease to exist—painlessly, silently, bloodlessly vanish, without mourning or regret. That was the unspoken fantasy with which I fell asleep each night. That was the one conceivable future that would allow the rest of us to flourish.

I couldn't keep the idea at bay. As guilty as it made me feel, it was there, and it kept asserting itself in my thoughts. Life was better without him. Every day confirmed that fact over and over again. And finally, I prayed, not for the reality of death, but that somehow—in some magical, acceptable way—he would never return to us. I prayed that he would be gone forever, a faded memory like the soiled photo of Ricky's father. He could become a glossy phantom in black and white, with a history that sprang only from my own imaginings.

I kept my shameful desire hidden, though Ricky may have been the one person who suspected and understood. We had each taken to collecting and trading marbles, and as we examined our collections one summer day in Ricky's front yard, I believe he guessed at my innermost wishes.

"Can I see your blue purie?" he asked.

"Sure." I handed him my prize marble.

Ricky held it close to his right eye and turned toward the

sun. Holding it between his thumb and forefinger, he rotated the marble slightly. He rolled it back and forth, his left eye shut, his mouth agape. "I'll give you two of my best cat's-eyes for this purie."

"Naw. I like my blue purie best of all my marbles."

"Yeah, it's really neat. How about two of my cat's-eyes and any one of my other marbles?"

"I don't want to trade, but, if you want, you can keep it for a couple of days."

"Really?"

"Sure."

He placed the blue marble in the colorful gathering spread before him on the grass. "Is your mom gone all day?"

"Yeah."

"Maybe we could go over to your place and look at these."

"That's not a good idea. The O'Neils are taking care of Katy, and they don't like lots of kids around."

"Oh." Ricky picked up the purie, stretched out on his back in the grass and held the marble toward the sun again. "She went to see your dad?" he asked pensively.

"Yeah. She took the bus to Willmar and she won't be back till tonight."

"Is he better?"

"I guess so."

"How come you and Ron didn't go?"

"I don't know. She said maybe next time we should go with her." I didn't tell Ricky that I didn't want to go—ever.

Ricky rolled onto his side and placed the marble back in his collection. "I wish I could go somewhere and see my dad." He smiled thinly, his eyes all distant and dreamy. "Wish I could just get on some old bus and when I got to the end my dad would be there. I wouldn't care what he did or if he was crabby or anything."

"Yeah. I know what you mean, but this is different."

Ricky blinked away the dreams in his eyes and squinted at me. "What do you mean?"

"I don't know. It's just different. He was awfully mean and stuff before he went away."

Ricky stared at me, giving no voice to whatever thoughts stirred behind his tiny blue eyes. He rolled onto his back again and looked up at the few stray clouds that dotted the summer sky. "Yeah, I guess it is different. Anyway, he'll be coming home, won't he?"

"Yeah. By the end of summer he'll be back. That's what my mom said anyway. She said he'll be back before we start school again."

"That's a long time, but at least you know he'll be coming home."

"Yeah."

"And maybe you'll get to go see him before he comes home. Maybe you'll get to go around Willmar with him and—"

"Ricky," I interrupted. "It's almost time to go help Ron with his route. Do you want to go with me or what?" I didn't intend for the words to come out so harshly, or to betray my anger, but they did.

Ricky stopped his cloud watching and rolled onto his side again. He plucked a blade of grass and chewed on the end of it. "You don't want to see him, do you?"

"What?"

"Your dad," he said, narrowing his eyes again and chewing on the grass. "You don't want to see him, do you?"

"I don't know," I said hurriedly. "Look, do you want to go with me on Ron's route?"

He chewed on his blade of grass and waited to answer. "I guess not today," he said. "I think I'll just stay here. Okay?"

"Sure. It's okay."

He discarded the blade of grass. "Maybe I'll see you after."

"Yeah. I'll see you after." I took my cigar box of marbles and got up to leave. "You can keep the purie as long as you want. Just keep it with your collection."

"Thanks."

"It's okay," I said. I lingered a moment, looking down on him and his array of marbles that speckled the lawn. "Well, I'll see ya later."

"Okay," he said.

I hurried down the embankment and across the avenue to my side of the street. I was about to break into a sprint toward home when I heard Ricky call out to me. "You're a lucky stiff!" he shouted. "Do you know that?" I just waved back and ran toward home.

Twenty-Three

Dad had been gone nearly a month before I saw him. I had balked at going, unwilling to face the source of so much pain and the confirmation of his inevitable return. Despite my protests, my mother's insistence won out. "He's still your father," she said. She didn't say any more. She didn't need to. With those few words I came to realize that Mom's allegiance to Dad had strengthened during his absence, while mine had dissipated. The more I thought about that, the more ashamed I felt about not wanting to go see him. And so the three of us went to Willmar, each with our own conflicting emotions and expectations.

We weren't allowed into the wards or the labyrinth of hallways that honeycombed the institution. Instead, we waited in a lounge area that seemed to have captured and intensified all the heat of the summer afternoon. The room was colored in drab green and browns with a single, enormous oil painting of a gray-haired man in a suit and tie. His eyes dominated the room. They penetrated anyone who dared to look at him, and admonished young boys who had shown the slightest reluctance about visiting their fathers.

Ron and I were seated on a couch, windows to our back, the painting of my nameless accuser on the wall to our right. Mom spoke to us, but I didn't listen. I was busy watching the only other occupants of the room, a man and woman who sat in a far corner facing one another, their heads lowered, their voices barely above a whisper. I watched them and wondered why they didn't look at each other. They leaned closer, so close I thought they would bump foreheads, and still they didn't look at each other. Dimly, I heard my mother. "Now, you two stay right here. I'll be back in a minute or two." She was gone and I sneaked another look at the painting of my steely-eyed judge.

"Where'd Mom go?" I whispered to Ron. It seemed appropriate to whisper.

"I don't know. To get Dad, I guess."

Ron seemed irritated, and I suddenly realized that he hadn't expressed his feelings about seeing Dad, at least not to me. I suspected that he was even more uncomfortable than I was with the visit, and I sensed it was best not to ask him about it. I slid back deep into the couch and watched the couple in the corner. I tried not to look at the painting again.

I watched the two strangers until I saw Mom smiling apprehensively and hurrying back toward Ron and me. "Your father will be down in a minute, boys. He's going to be so happy that you're both here. Try not to be nervous." Her advice was to us, but I felt she was coaching herself as well. "Remember," she said, looking at us intently, "your father loves you both very much. I know that we've had some bad times, but he's sorry for all of what's happened and he just wants us to be a family again. I know that he wants you both to . . ." Her voice faded away and she began over. "He's much better, boys. He feels terrible about the troubles we've had, and he needs to know that you both still love him."

Ron looked away, unwilling or unable to say whatever words she wanted so much to hear. I glanced at the painting of my stern-faced judge. "Sure, Mom," I said.

She turned and looked at the elevator doors that faced the lounge, hesitated, then looked again at Ron and me. "Do I look all right?"

"You look fine, Mom," Ron said sullenly.

"Well, I just want us all to—" She stopped at the sound of the elevator opening.

My father was the only one to exit the yawning doors. He wore a light blue bathrobe and slippers, and the moment I saw him I was overcome with guilt. Now, walking toward me, thin and pale and sober, was the man I had prayed would cease to exist. But this was not the raging drunk who had terrorized my mother and haunted my dreams. This was not the man who stole his son's paper route money and tried to destroy his family's home. And yet, it *was* him. It was my father.

My mother went to him. They stood close and held hands, but they didn't kiss. She whispered something to him and he nodded. They parted, put their arms around each other's backs, and walked side by side toward Ron and me.

Ron and I stood as they approached, and in my shame I couldn't look up at him.

"Thanks for coming to see me, boys," he said.

"Sure," Ron said.

I mumbled something incoherent.

"How have you boys been? Ron?"

"Good. Everything's okay."

"Michael? I've missed you. Are you being good for your mom?"

"Sure," I managed to get out, but still I couldn't look at him.

"Well, maybe we could all sit down here and talk a little. You boys can tell me how your summer is going."

He stepped away to retrieve a chair, and Mom took the opportunity to whisper to Ron and me. "Tell him it's good to see him, and that you've missed him."

"It isn't true," Ron said, but low enough so that our mom couldn't hear him.

He returned, sliding a chair toward the couch to form a conversation nook. He sat down and leaned forward, resting his elbows just above his knees. Mom sat on the couch near him, then Ron, and finally me. "So," he said, groping for words, "you all look so good. I've missed you. And Katy, how's little Katy?"

"Oh, she's just great, Pat," my mother said. "The O'Neils are taking care of her today." She spoke quickly, her words rushed and full of anxiety. "We've all missed you. We'll all be so glad when things are . . . when you're home again."

"Yeah," he said slowly and looked at the floor. He reached into a pocket of his robe and took out a lighter and a crumpled pack of Camels. He leaned back to light his cigarette and for the first time I noticed that his hands were shaking. The flame of the lighter flickered and jumped as he tried to steady it with both hands.

"Would you like me to help you light that, Pat?" my mother said.

"I'm fine," he snarled. Then, more gently, "Sorry, no, I'm fine. I'll get it here in a second. Afraid I'm not too steady these days." He forced a mild laugh.

I looked at his face. I don't think I'd ever heard him apologize to my mother before, or ever heard him joke about his own ineptitude. And when I looked at him, the most remarkable thing happened. Our eyes met—just his and mine—and for a moment there was no one else in that lounge. Ron and Mom were as distant as the faintest star in the heavens. No one whispered in the far corners of the room, and there was no painting staring down at me from the wall. There was only my dad's face, and those pale eyes so full of pain and remorse. I was sure he was going to say something to me, but he only smiled weakly and looked at me. Then it happened, that haunting, fleeting instant when tears gathered to his eyes, and he looked away. He set his cigarette in an ashtray next to his chair and wiped his face with both hands. He cleared his throat twice and began to talk of when he would come home and how his job on the road would still be there for him.

But, I had seen it. In his eyes, in that transitory speck of time I had seen what he couldn't bring himself to say. And I understood, because at that precise moment I had wanted to say the same thing myself. I had wanted to ask of him what his eyes cried out—"Forgive me!"

Twenty-four

Katy's birthday and the Fourth of July came shortly after our visit to Willmar. Both celebrations made me think of my father, my feelings now confused by the image of a shaken, sober, contrite man. At Katy's party, I thought of the previous year and the ruined dinner and choking down cold spaghetti and cake. Then, as the fear and resentment rose in me, that memory was replaced by the vision of the slender man in a blue robe, unable to express whatever torment and regret he felt. Life was peaceful now, but I still had no way of knowing what might happen when he finally returned to us, no way of making sense of the web of my own feelings. And so I tried again not to think of him at all. Whether he should be pitied or condemned was a riddle I could not solve, and I welcomed those moments of distraction when he was beyond my awareness and my guilt.

Mom said that she was going to take Ron and Ricky and me to Powderhorn Park for the carnival and fireworks. If we left as soon as Ron was done with his paper route, we could spend most of the afternoon at the carnival and stay to see the fireworks after dark. She had saved tip money to treat all of us to a real holiday.

Powderhorn was several miles south and east of where we lived, reachable by a short ride on the streetcar. The north end of the park was a natural valley, its grassy slopes ideally suited for sledding and tobogganing in winter. To the south, a small, placid lake with a single island provided an enormous skating rink. In summer, the lake, unfit for swimming or fishing, served as little more than pleasant scenery. It was infested with leeches and rumored to be bottomless. But, on the Fourth of July, it became purposeful once again. The island became a launch site for spectacular fireworks, the colorful explosions reflected in the shimmering water.

On the southeastern corner of the lake was a gray stucco pavilion and a dirt lot large enough to accommodate a carnival with a Ferris wheel, a merry-go-round, kiddy cars that moved in slow, endless circles, a miniature roller coaster, and a thrilling new ride called the tilt-a-whirl. There were concessions, too—brightly colored wagons of red and yellow that sold Cracker Jack and hot dogs and cotton candy and soft drinks.

The crowds swarmed around the mechanized excitement, raising dust clouds that mingled with the odor of hot dogs and popcorn and the multitude itself. Impatient lines formed at every ticket booth, jostling each other and chattering. Now and then, rising above the drone of the machinery and the crowd, there was the rapid *popping* of firecrackers. This was followed by dramatic shrieks of young girls and the deep laughter of men.

Ron and Ricky and I waited in line for the tilt-a-whirl and watched those already swinging in circles of fright. Each car contained a bench seat wide enough to hold three people. The front of the car was open, while the metal frame rose behind and above the riders' heads like the hood of a giant cobra. Each car spun freely in its own circular track, and the entire platform on which the cars rode also rotated. Spinning circles within a spinning circle—controlled chaos at its absolute finest!

A sense of freedom overwhelmed me. I looked around at the swirling colors of the rides, the happy faces, the grand celebration of which we were a part. We were free to roam the grounds, free to make the most dazzling choices. This was a holiday at its best.

"When we get in our car, let me sit on the outside," Ron instructed. "I weigh more than you guys, and if I sit on the outside I can get it spinning better."

I didn't understand the theory, but I trusted his judgment. "Okay," I said.

Ricky was watching the people in the cars, his mouth ajar. As the ride reached its maximum velocity, the cars roared past us, drowning out the screams and laughter of the riders.

"See that one?" Ron shouted and pointed to the only car that was rotating a complete three hundred and sixty degrees. "That's what we want ours to do. We wanna get that thing really going."

"Right," I said.

Ricky didn't answer.

As the great platform slowed, the arc of the swinging cars diminished.

Ricky and I watched the car that had been spinning so wildly. It came near us, and I could see that there were only two people in it—an obese boy about Ron's age and a girl of eight or nine years that I assumed to be his sister. As the car drew closer, I noticed that the boy looked oddly disturbed. His face was pale, his eyes glazed and lifeless. I kept watching his face until the car he rode in came to a halt in front us. Suddenly, explosively, my puzzlement was answered. With great *urping* sounds, the boy brought up the bilious contents of his stomach. It spewed out over his chest and onto his lap. Once, twice, three times in horrible succession.

"God, Ron!" I shouted. "That fat kid is puking all over himself."

Ron turned to witness the scene that Ricky and I watched in frozen horror.

"Duck," Ron shouted and pulled both of us down below the level of the platform. The obese boy was doing what must have seemed to him the only rational thing to do. He was ridding himself of the mess, scraping up handfuls of the disgorged matter and flinging it out into the crowd. There were scattered shouts of "What the hell!" and "Jesus Christ!" as the warm, moist particles struck unsuspecting victims.

In the shadow of the platform, crouched safely out of the range of the disgusting barrage, Ricky said, "Let's not go on this ride."

"Aw, come on, Ricky," Ron said. "You won't get sick like that. Did you see how fat that kid was? He probably ate fifty hot dogs before he got on the ride."

"I don't know, Ron. I don't feel so good myself right now," Ricky said.

"Come on, we're next in line." There was a moment of silence and then a compromise offered by Ron. "Look, we won't get our car swinging that much. Okay? What do you say, Ricky?"

"Okay, but don't make it go all the way around."

The three of us stood to climb the steps that led to the platform and the cars, with Ron in the lead. He looked back over his shoulder to give us a final instruction. "We won't sit in the car that fat kid was in."

"Right," I said.

We survived the tilt-a-whirl, and even found the courage to ride it a second time before the summer afternoon faded to dusky twilight. The lights of the rides were turned on—a million tiny bulbs that outlined and defined the carnival and made it sparkle like a living, pulsating jewel in the summer evening. The three of us stood near one of the concession stands, basking in the warm magic of the gathering darkness.

"It won't be long till they start the fireworks," Ron said. "We better go find Mom up on the hill." He nodded toward the grassy, treeless hillside that served as a natural amphitheater for the display. It was already crowded with eager spectators, some lounging on blankets, others meandering up and down the hill seeking the best vantage point.

"Yeah, let's go, Mike," Ricky said. "We don't want to miss anything."

I was about to answer when the sounds of a scuffle erupted behind me. I turned and backed instinctively toward Ron and Ricky, away from the tumult.

There were two men moving quickly, their arms thickly muscled and glistening in the glow of the carnival lights. Then I saw a third man that they were pushing and shoving through the crowd. There were sounds of scraping feet and shouts of struggle—the familiar sounds of fighting. "Get the hell out of here!" one of the pushers yelled. "You don't pull that crap around here. Go on, get the hell out of the park! Go home and sleep it off, you goddamn drunk!"

The drunk broke free of the two men and threw a wild punch. One of the pushers grabbed the drunk's arm and twisted it behind his back. The silenced crowd parted, then sealed up again behind the three of them.

"What happened?" I said to no one. My heart was pounding and I felt nauseated.

"I don't know. They were sure mad at that guy for something," Ricky answered.

"Come on. Let's go, you guys. Forget that stuff. It's over," Ron said sullenly.

As we headed for the hill, the two men who had removed the drunk from the park were headed back toward the carnival and crossed our path. "Goddamn drunks," one said to the other and shook his head in disgust.

———

Later, as we sat on the grassy hillside and watched the night sky being illuminated by glowing, twinkling canopies of gold and green and blue, I thought of the man ejected from the park, and of my father. The *ooohs* and *aaahs* of the crowd were remote and without meaning. Even the booming salutes that shook the tiny island and raced across the water to reverberate in a thousand heaving chests could not touch me. I was beyond the short-lived joy of the evening, reminded now of the fragile, tenuous nature of my happiness. The holiday had been lost—lost in the terrible knowledge that without reason or warning what is beautiful can become brutish, lost in the belief that in all faith and elation lies the capacity for disappointment and despair.

Twenty-Five

Ron and I didn't go to see our father again that summer. I don't know why. We simply weren't asked to go. Maybe it was because of money, or because it was more comfortable for our mother to see him without us, or because we expressed no desire to join her. In any event, we didn't go back to Willmar, and the fact that he would eventually return to our home became more and more of an abstraction.

I was busy that summer. There was Ron's paper route to do, and swapping marbles with Ricky, and taking care of Katy. There were outings to Elliot Park, where we swam throughout the long, languid summer afternoons. Sunday mornings meant church with the O'Neils and stopping at Bierman's for ice cream. There were no movies, but on some mornings my mother was able to give Ricky and me a little change from her tip money, which was good for a trip to Rotograph's and Ralph and Jack's Grocery. And there were cap gun fights.

Ricky helped with Ron's route whenever he could, and instead of spending money on penny candy, he saved what Ron gave him until he was able to buy a cap gun. It wasn't as fancy as mine, but it was his—earned through his own efforts. I knew that he cherished it almost as much as the book his father had given him and the photograph he had once shown me. It was strange, knowing how much he loved that gun, that he never took it home. When the last desperado had fallen in the late-afternoon sun, he always asked me to take it home and keep it safe for him. I never asked him why he didn't keep it at his house. I had come to accept these little oddities—maybe in the same way that I accepted the fact that he never took off his T-shirt when we went swimming.

I saw Leo almost daily that summer, always keeping his vigil at the ice house. I now thought of him as a friend and protector and his rambling conversation and questions, once so annoying, had become a comfort. There were, however, aspects of his personality that remained a mystery to me. His sudden bursts of laughter when he spoke with Ricky and me were unfathomable, often coming at the most serious point of our conversation. And he was always grinning, as if he knew some great secret that he couldn't or wouldn't share with us. Ricky and I simply couldn't see why Leo found us so amusing. But, other than those little eccentricities, it was always good to see him and tell him about our day. Adults, I concluded, more often than not, had some bizarre slant to their personalities. No matter how normal and stable and intelligent they appeared, sooner or later they revealed some strange belief or flaw in their character.

Sometimes their impaired thinking was immediately apparent, as it was with Mr. Flaherty. I knew almost nothing about the man, except that he lived alone on the third floor of our building and was retired from the railroad. He was almost always among the adults on the front steps on rainy day gatherings. He was thin and gray and his clothes forever looked dusty to me, as if he lived among antique chairs and trunks in some forgotten attic.

Mr. Flaherty gained unaccustomed attention that summer because of all the people who lived in our building he was the sole owner of a new luxury called a television. I understood that television was like a radio with living pictures. It was like having a tiny movie theater in your home.

I had never spoken with Mr. Flaherty, but like everyone else in the building, I knew who he was and what he owned. Late one afternoon he sat alone on the front steps, looking all gray and silent and dusty in the long shadows of our building. Ricky and I were on the walk in front of him, bringing to a close our cap gun drama of the day. Unexpectedly, Mr. Flaherty called out to us.

"You boys ever listen to *The Lone Ranger* on radio?"

"Sure," we answered together.

"Well, he's on television. I see him every week on my television."

"You do?" I said.

"Yes sir. Just like he is on the radio."

I waited and hoped that he would ask Ricky and me if we would like to watch the show with him sometime, but he didn't say anything. Ricky and I looked at each other and I wondered what to say next to keep the opportunity from slipping away. "What does he look like?" I shouted excitedly to Mr. Flaherty.

"He looks just the way you imagine him," he called back. Then he laughed a high laugh. I could almost see dust rising up from his neck and shoulders as he shook with mirth. He stood, climbed to the archway at the top of the steps and turned back toward Ricky and me. "Yup," he said, cackling, "he looks just exactly the way you imagine him." He laughed again and vanished into the building.

"How does he know that?"

"What?" Ricky said.

"How does he know what I imagine?"

"I don't think he can," Ricky said thoughtfully.

We never got to see *The Lone Ranger,* but it didn't really detract from those treasured days and nights that led inexorably to autumn and school and my father's return. It was our golden season of prolonged tranquillity that I thought would never end. It was our time to grow, roam, dream, create, sleep deeply through many nights. Perhaps, because it seemed the summer would go on forever, it could be said that we failed to appreciate it—but that would be wrong. Instead, the days were not shackled by an awareness of time and limitations, and an end. It was *our* moment, unbounded and enduring.

Then, without warning, one dewy August morning, with just over a week until school was to begin, we prepared for my father's return. The day began at seven. Mom wanted the normally clean apartment to be immaculate. Ron and I were dispatched on a variety of chores, or entertained Katy while Mom polished floors, swept, scoured the bathroom twice, and cleaned every window and mirror in the place. She scurried around, giving directions, arranging and rearranging rugs and placemats and ashtrays, agonizing over the tiniest detail until the entire place seemed to glow from her incredible expenditure of energy.

At four that afternoon she left with the O'Neils to meet Dad at the Greyhound depot, but not before she had conducted a final inspection of the three of us and all of the apartment. In the final flurry of her exiting, she gave us instructions and asked questions, not waiting for any response or answer. "Keep Katy clean . . . no visitors until we get back . . . you can eat something if you're hungry, but clean up afterward . . . do I look all right?"

Finally, with the O'Neils waiting at the door, she knelt down in front of Ron and Katy and me, sitting solemnly on the couch. "I'll be back in less than an hour. Be good while I'm gone. When I get back, your father will be with me."

Katy wiggled and turned her head away, burying her face in the safety of a sofa cushion.

Mom put her hands on Katy's shoulders and turned her face-forward. "He loves you all," she said and scanned us with her eyes. "I want you to welcome him back. I want you to let him know that we've forgi—" She stopped, blinked her eyes, and patted her hair. When she spoke again, her voice was softer, less pressured. "Everything will be much different now, you'll see." She smiled, her eyes both sad and infinitely hopeful. "I've got to go now. I love you all so much." She pulled each of us forward, one at a time, and kissed us on the forehead. When she was done, she rose and went to the O'Neils. Before they left, she turned to wave to us from the doorway.

———

Just as Mom promised, within an hour they returned. As if by decree from some precise inner clock, the three of us had returned to the couch, to the very positions we had occupied when she left.

We heard muffled voices, then the door to the apartment opened. Dad entered first, with Mom close behind. He looked smaller to me than I remembered—as he had at the hospital. But, he was not so pale, not sickly looking as when I'd last seen him. He wore a powder-blue shirt I'd never seen before, the long sleeves rolled back to the elbow. He stepped into the apartment, advancing only a few steps toward the couch. He carefully placed a black overnight bag on the floor and looked at us, as if he were bewildered. Behind him, Mom motioned to us to come forward and welcome him back.

"Hi, kids," he said, his voice delicate and unfamiliar. "It's good to see you all again . . . to be home."

Katy squealed and buried her face in the couch. Ron hung his head and said nothing. I looked beyond my father and saw my mother, pleading with her gestures for us to come forward.

Without thought or reflection, I broke the awkward silence.

"Dad!" I shouted and ran to him. He bent forward and caught me up in his arms. His face was smooth-shaven and warm against my cheek and he smelled all soapy-fresh. "Michael, Michael . . . ," he said over and over.

Behind me, I could hear Ron and Katy as they left the couch to join us. "Welcome home, Dad," Ron said stiffly. Katy jumped and squealed, "Home Dad! Home Dad!"

Soon we were all huddled in a tearful embrace, fulfilling at least for the moment some tiny part of my mother's dream. But, even before the circle was broken, I sensed that we had come to the end of something. It was the end of our summer interlude, and in a larger sense of something I could not name.

Twenty-Six

Nothing had changed and yet nothing was the same. For weeks there was a cautious air about our home, a sort of clumsy, fragile politeness as we all adjusted to my father's presence. Nothing was said about the past or his commitment to Willmar—at least not to us children. We tried to act as if none of it had ever happened, but I noticed that my parents had quiet conversations that ended abruptly when Ron or I entered the room, and evenings they went out, just the two of them strolling slowly through the neighborhood in the early autumn nights. Sometimes, as I watched them walk away through the long corridor of elm trees that lined the street, he would put his arm around her shoulders, or take hold of her hand. I don't know what they talked about; I only know that they were closer than I had ever seen them and that I began to gain a sense of security in their rediscovery of each other.

The tension that previously had filled our home whenever Dad was around had disappeared. He no longer conveyed that desperate, explosive presence that previously had kept us all on edge. Even Ron noticed the change. "Dad doesn't seem so mad anymore." That was how he said it, and I knew exactly what he meant. And, one night, as I pretended to be asleep on the couch and listened to my parents' muted conversation, I heard my father say, "I think they're all right, don't you?" I knew he was talking about Ron and Katy and me. Then I heard him whisper, "Oh, Jean, how could I have done the things I did?" I heard it and I believed he had changed. Maybe, I thought, just maybe, we would never return to those nightmarish days.

Ricky and I spent more time in my house, now that the evenings were chilled by the winds of fall and there was a true calm in our house. One Wednesday, just before dinner, we were stretched out on the floor in front of the old Philco radio. Frank Sinatra was singing "I'll Be Seeing You," but we weren't listening. We were busy looking at comics while my parents talked in the kitchen as my mother cooked. I was just about to see how Tubby would extricate himself from some impossible dilemma when my mother came into the room.

"Ricky, would you like to stay and have dinner with us?"

He didn't answer. He turned toward me, his eyes sharp and full of surprise. He gave me a quick nod. "That'd be great, Mom," I said.

He turned toward her and looked up. "Sure, thanks."

My mother smiled. "You're welcome, Ricky. We'll be eating in a few minutes."

Ricky sprang to his feet. "But I've got to ask my mom if it's okay."

"Would you like me to call her?" my mother said.

"Sure." He stood a little longer, then dropped down beside me on the floor. "Hope I can stay," he said. "Maybe we could look at more comics after we eat. You must have a million of them."

"Sure, we can look at more of them," I said and smiled.

Within a few minutes my mother returned. She looked pale and somber, almost frightened. "I'm . . . I'm afraid Ricky can't stay for dinner. You're supposed to go home right away. Your mother was . . . she seemed upset."

Ricky was already on his feet, pulling on his jacket.

"I'm sorry, Ricky," she said. "I wish you could have stayed. Maybe another time."

"Sure," he said as he hurried toward the door. "Thanks anyway."

"See ya tomorrow," I shouted.

"Yeah, see ya," he said without looking back. The door closed and he was gone.

"Well," my mother said, still looking at the door and not fully composed, "you can come and eat now, Michael."

For at least half an hour I had had a strange sense of unrest. I felt flushed and in that border state of entertaining and denying the possibility of illness. Now, as I stood up, I felt dizzy and weak. I headed toward the kitchen and conducted little experiments to discover the nature and limits of this sudden malaise. I turned my head from side to side. I stretched. I moved my eyes back and forth. "Mom, it hurts when I do this."

"What?"

I stood behind her at the stove, bathed in the rich aroma of onions and potatoes frying in a pan. Somehow, the thought of eating no longer appealed to me. "My head hurts when I do this," I said and rolled my eyes in painful orbits.

She put down the pan she had just picked up off the stove and wiped her hands on her apron. "Come here, Michael."

She held me close to her and pressed a hand to my forehead. "Pat, would you get the thermometer for me? I think Michael may have a fever."

My temperature was one hundred and two degrees. I knew that anything over one hundred meant a call to Dr. Rosen. In less than an hour he was at our house. Thin and taciturn and methodical, the little doctor checked my ears and eyes and throat. He prodded my abdomen with his skinny fingers and monotonously repeated, "Does that hurt?" He looked at me over his glasses and asked about what I had eaten and where I'd been playing and when I first noticed that I didn't feel well. At last, he gave me a long, serious look, patted me on the shoulder, and said, "I'm sure you'll be well in a few days. I've got to talk with your mom and dad now."

I strained to hear what the three of them were saying. From his grainy black bag, Dr. Rosen produced a dark bottle of medicine that I knew would taste horrible. He gave some brief instructions to my parents, but still I heard no diagnosis. More important, and of greater interest than the nature of my illness, I did hear him say, "I'd keep him out of school for a few days, or at least until the fever is gone and he's feeling strong again."

After he left, Mom did everything possible to make me comfortable. I was ensconced on the couch, my cap gun at my side, several pillows behind my head, and a wealth of comic books at hand. Next to the couch, within easy reach, she had placed a chair with a water glass, a pitcher, and a bowl of ice chips. She encouraged me to drink as much water as I could tolerate. I had only eaten a little Jell-O for dinner, my appetite not running much toward solid food. I was assured that anything I wanted was mine simply for the asking. There was a cool cloth on my forehead that was changed at regular intervals and I was advised, as I already knew, that school was out of the question. My only duty was to rest and get well as soon as possible. So, with my discomfort greatly relieved by all the attention and my own inactivity, I settled in for a recovery that I hoped would take at least until the weekend. It was all perfect, except for Ron, who whispered, "Faker," when he said good night to me.

———

I slept late the next morning and didn't even hear Ron leave for school. I probably would have slept even longer if it hadn't been for my parents' agitation. They were trying to keep their voices down, but they woke me as they stood at our front window trying to figure out what all the excitement was about on the street.

"There are at least two squad cars out there," Dad said as he strained his neck for the maximum view out the basement window.

"My God, Pat, I think they must be at Ricky's house," Mom said.

I was shocked fully awake when I heard Ricky's name.

"Are the kids asleep?" Mom asked.

"I think so. Why?"

"I have a terrible feeling about this, Pat. I want to go over there and find out what's happened."

"The kids will be all right. Just hang on a second and I'll go with you."

As the two of them headed for the door, I turned on my side and shouted at them—or tried to. I discovered my throat was sore, and in my effort to shout, I produced only a kind of croaking sound that went unnoticed. I made a second attempt, which failed as well.

The fact that both of them left the apartment frightened me. It wasn't fear of being alone, but fear that whatever was so compelling to cause them to leave must be something of unprece-

dented, possibly terrifying dimensions. And they had mentioned
Ricky. My mother had said she thought the police were at Ricky's
house.

I sat up and felt a throbbing sensation behind my eyes. I
waited until the pain diminished to a tolerable level. I put on my
shoes, no socks, and slipped a jacket on over my pajamas. My
legs were shaky and the room appeared to vibrate and defy my
attempts to keep it in steady focus. I leaned against the front
door to gather strength to climb the stairs to the main entrance.

When I got up to the archway that opened onto Elliot Avenue, the early morning sun struck with a vengeance. The pain
behind my eyes sprang to life. I squinted and held my hand,
salute-style, protectively over my eyes. As I adjusted to the light,
I became aware of the dry, chilled air that turned the leather of
my shoes into icy wrappings on my sockless feet.

I looked down the street toward Ricky's house. There were
two police cars, an ambulance, and a crowd of people milling
around on the boulevard and among the parked vehicles. From
where I stood, I couldn't see my parents in the crowd or tell what
had happened. I slowly negotiated the cold stone steps and
started toward Ricky's.

As I walked along the pavement, the morning wind stung
my cheeks and brought a watery film to my eyes. With each step,
I felt a growing sense of dread and an awareness of my own
heartbeat. It thundered in my chest, hard and wild with fear. My
breath came quicker, little puffs of vapor appearing in the air
each time I exhaled. The smell of early autumn—drying leaves
and mown grass—filled my nostrils. I glanced up the street. The
red cross on the ambulance was as bright and luminous as fresh
blood. When I reached the crowd, it was as if I really wasn't there
at all. I moved through them and around them, unnoticed as I
worked my way toward my friend's house.

"Both of them," I heard a woman say. "He was under his bed," someone else said. "My God, it's just terrible. I knew she was crazy, but I never thought she'd do something like this."

I continued to snake my way through the crowd, moving past people with the ease of the morning wind. To me, they were motionless now. Women in housedresses hugged themselves against the cold. A few men in work jackets and khaki pants and unpolished work boots stood with their faces wrinkled and distorted. I didn't know them. They were all strangers—curious, mumbling, gawking strangers.

"I guess he tried to stop the bleeding with socks," a voice said. "He was under his bed with some book—all curled up with some book."

"She'd turned the gas on, too," a man added.

I had made my way to the front of the crowd. And then I saw it. Two men, one backing down the steps, moving gingerly, the other walking forward. Between them was a stretcher, and a small form covered by a white sheet. A gust of wind lifted one end of the sheet for just an instant. But in that moment, as the sheet flapped once in the breeze, I saw it. A triangular patch of hair—flaming and unmistakable.

"Nooo!" I screamed, and the base of my skull pulsed with pain in response. "Ricky!" I cried, my voice shrill and foreign to my own ears. "Ricky! Nooo!"

My mother's voice came out of the crowd. "My God, Pat, it's Michael!"

Strong arms swept me up. I struggled and screamed Ricky's name over and over in the indifferent autumn air. I fought against restraint, without any idea of what I might do if I broke free. I fought against what I had seen, against the strength of my father's arms, against the horror I could not change or accept, against my own pain, and, finally, against nothing at all.

Twenty-Seven

There was a service for Ricky and his mother, but I didn't go to it. It was held on Saturday, and I was still sick. Even if I had been well, I don't know if I would have gone, or been allowed to go. Ron and my parents went to it while Mrs. O'Neil stayed with Katy and me. I gave Ricky's cap gun to my mom, and she promised to see that it was buried with him. When they got home, I could tell they had all been crying—even my dad. They pretended they hadn't. They spoke too loudly about what we might have for dinner, and what time Ron needed to leave for his route, and whether or not it might rain. I could tell they were trying not to think about it, and that they were trying to keep me from thinking about it, too.

Mrs. Stedman hadn't even left a note. No one knew or would ever know what tormented thoughts had driven her to take her own life and the life of her son. I suppose, in a way, that it didn't matter. All anyone could ever really understand was that somewhere, within a twisted set of rules, dark voices had spoken to her that no one else could hear or understand. And she had obeyed. In those last tortured moments she had followed those deluded commands, laying open her son's wrists and her own.

To the end, Ricky had struggled against that darkness. He had retreated to his room. There, beneath his bed, clinging to his book—to his symbol and dream of love—he had tried to stop the bleeding. Reaching out for that one bright remembrance, he had remained there until all life had slipped away. There was no explanation. There could be no explanation. There was only the unalterable reality of what had happened, and the aching, enigmatic sadness and beauty of his little life.

I recovered from my illness, but my brooding over Ricky's death became an even greater concern to my parents. Ron did all he could to distract me and make me laugh, but he couldn't really help. None of them could, because they hadn't seen the things I'd seen. They didn't know what I knew. Even Dr. Rosen was called. He talked to me and to my parents. He spoke of another doctor who might be able to help me with my problems. They all went about fretting and worrying and not understanding.

Most of all, I think none of them could understand why I had never cried about it. They kept trying to get me to tell them how I felt, but there was no way to describe my sense of loss, or reveal the secret I kept locked deep inside myself.

Each morning, as I walked alone to school, I would look across the street at Ricky's house. It was dark and foreboding. The house and yard seemed as changed and lifeless as the barren trees along the boulevard. After a while, I stopped looking at it. When I left our building, I'd cut back to the alley and avoid going past Ricky's altogether. It didn't really help, though, because I thought about him constantly. I wondered if maybe none of it would have happened if only he hadn't made me promise not to tell about the beatings. Or maybe, if he could have stayed for dinner that night, somehow that would have made a difference.

It was impossible to concentrate at school, too. I tried to pay attention to my teacher, but pretty soon I'd be thinking about Ricky and the things we'd done together and I wouldn't know what she was talking about. Everyone knew about Ricky, but they didn't say anything about it. Just once, when class ended, my teacher came to me and said, "Michael, I know that you're having a lot of difficulty with your studies these days. Would you like to talk about it with me?" I just shrugged and waited until she left me alone. The only other person who said anything at all was Larry Olson. He stopped me after school, almost in the exact spot where we had fought. He stood in front of me looking embarrassed and uncertain. His face was all red and he looked like he wanted to be somewhere else, but he managed to get out what he had to tell me. "I'm sorry about—you know." His face grew so red it looked like it might explode. "Anyway, I'm really sorry," he said, then he turned and ran away.

Ron was less troubled about it, or so it appeared. Maybe it was because he was older, or because he hadn't been there the morning they took Ricky away, or because he didn't know the secret. But he had been Ricky's friend, too, and he talked about how much he missed him and how terrible it all had been. "He was a great kid," he said one afternoon as we delivered papers. "Remember the night we raided the bar and he didn't know how to whistle?"

"Sure." I felt my throat grow hot and thick. I couldn't say anything more.

"That was funny."

"Yeah."

"I really miss him. He was a great kid."

That was how Ron dealt with it. Openly, matter-of-factly, without hesitation, he revealed to you what was on his mind and what bothered him. That was his way.

It was nearly two weeks after Ricky's death that I finally told my mother. Everyone had gone to bed for the night and as I lay awake on the couch listening to the soft tapping of autumn rain against the window, she came to me.

"Michael, are you awake?" she whispered.

"Yeah," I whispered back.

"Honey, what is it? Isn't there something I can do to help?" She knelt beside the couch and draped her arms across my chest.

"I knew she was being mean to him," I said. I had to tell it all. I couldn't hold back any longer.

"What?"

"Ricky showed me once, but he made me promise not to ever tell anyone."

Mom leaned close and brushed my hair from my eyes. She smelled all clean and fresh, and her hand was warm and soft against my forehead. "What did he show you?"

"One time he showed me his back. It had all these marks where she hit him 'cause he didn't pray good enough. But he told me not to ever tell anyone, and I promised I wouldn't."

"She hit him because he didn't pray well?"

"Yeah. He showed me. He said no matter how hard he tried, it was never good enough. We were out back behind the building one day, and he lifted up his shirt and showed me where she hit him. His back was all red and stuff, but he made me promise to never tell."

"Oh, Michael, is that what this is all about? You think now that you should have broken your promise and told someone about it? You think it might have changed things?"

"Yeah," I said, and it all burst forth. For the first time since that devastating morning, I cried. It came out in great, agonizing sobs until I could hardly breathe. Through it all, Mom rocked me in her arms and whispered my name over and over again.

Finally, she leaned back and looked at me. "It's not right to think you did something wrong. You couldn't have known. There was no way you could know. Ricky's mom was very sick—in her mind. We all knew that, but no one guessed she would do such a terrible thing. You were being his friend, that's all. You did what you thought was right. You were his best friend. All you ever gave him was happiness."

She hugged me and I began to cry again. I cried for Ricky and for myself and for the tragedy that defied all logic.

In the darkness, I saw Dad come out of the bedroom. He came and stood behind Mom. "Is Michael all right?" he whispered.

"I think so. I think he's going to be fine."

I choked out my darkest fear. "You'd never do anything like that, would you?"

"Oh, Michael," she sighed, "I love you and Ron and Katy so much. I can't even tell you how much. My heart is so full of love for all of you that sometimes I think it will break with happiness. And I will go on loving you all my life, nothing can ever change that. I will do all I ever can to keep you from harm—everything in my power." She stroked my hair and leaned close. In the darkness, I could see that there were tears in her eyes. Outside the rain fell harder now, and I could hear it beating relentlessly against our window. "Nothing can change my love for my children—nothing. And that love means that I could never do anything to hurt you."

In the darkness, out of the shadows, I heard my father whisper, "It's true."

Epilogue

The night I revealed Ricky's secret to my parents, I felt that a line had been crossed and that my world had been altered profoundly and forever. In the telling, I came to realize more fully the weight and finality of what had happened. As I drifted off to sleep, listening to the uneven rhythm of the rain against the window and the reassuring sound of my mother's voice, I knew that I would awaken to a place that was less innocent and less beautiful than it used to be. There was a luster to life—that indescribable radiance we experience only too briefly—that now would never return. My friend was gone.

The close of the 1940s brought the beginning and end of many things. In 1951, we left Elliot Avenue and moved to a house a few miles south of Franklin. It had three bedrooms, an unattached garage, and a small backyard with a weeping willow tree. It was, by any reasonable standards, a better place to live. But I missed our old apartment on Elliot, despite all the troubles we had known there. The O'Neils came to visit us a few times, but after a while we didn't see them anymore. I missed them. I

missed going to Rotograph's and Ralph and Jack's. I missed Leo.
I think I even missed Tiny.

There were, of course, new friends and a new school and a
more ordered way of life. For the first two years or so, I thought
the old problems had vanished from our lives. But that wasn't
the case. My father's drinking began again. It started slowly and
unobtrusively. It continued until all the old patterns—and the
abuse and fighting and horror—returned.

Mom acted more quickly than before, and Dad was com-
mitted to treatment for a second time. When he was released,
Ron was seventeen and I was thirteen. While Mom stayed with
him as she had before, the toll had been too much for Ron. I
think he had stopped believing in any hope for a permanent
change much earlier, but at seventeen there was finally a chance
for escape. So, he left on the road he saw open to himself. There
was the army—and the war in Korea.

How much weight can be given to anyone's action as an
influence on our lives I really can't say. I only know that Ron
leaving for Korea touched my father deeply. When Ron's letters
always came addressed only to my mother, I know that it hurt
him. He never drank again after that second commitment. But
in some ways his sobriety came too late, because the youth of his
children could never be recaptured, and so much of it had been
spent in so much pain.

Ron survived the war and came back decorated with a Bronze
Star for bravery. It didn't surprise me. In some ways I felt he had
been preparing himself for battle all his life. He didn't return to
Minnesota immediately. Instead, he settled in California, in the
San Francisco area. He stayed there for nearly five years, working for a car rental agency, and later for an investment firm. He
came home to us at Christmas twice during those years and

managed an uneasy peace with our father. While he lived in California, he met and married a woman from the Midwest. In 1959, he returned to Minneapolis, where he and his wife raised two sons.

Katy, maybe because she was the youngest, seemed to carry fewer scars from those early, turbulent years. She grew up beautiful and bright and untroubled. She left college in her sophomore year to marry a law student. Today, he is a successful trial lawyer in Chicago, where he and Katy and their daughter live in luxury that is nearly always sane and inoffensive. She and her family visit Minnesota at least once every year, usually during the holidays.

Unlike Ron and Katy, I never left the area. My wife and I live in a suburb just west of Minneapolis. The old neighborhood—or where it once existed—is less than half an hour away by car. Despite that, since the day we moved away from Elliot Avenue, I've only been back to that part of the city once. I went there on the first of July in 1960, the summer of the year I turned twenty. I wanted to keep my part of the pact I had made as a child. It was, I suppose, not a rational thing to do. There was no one to meet and no one to know if I kept my part of the bargain. Perhaps it was nothing more than some illogical sentiment that drove me there, or enduring regrets about what I might have done or what might have been. But it felt right—and it felt necessary.

Leo's ice house was gone, along with the building where we had lived. What had once been Rotograph's drugstore was a used clothing shop, and there were buses along Chicago Avenue instead of streetcars. All of it had changed, yet it brought back so many memories with so much painful intensity that I knew I would never return to that spot again. As I walked along the streets, thinking back to those lost boyhood days, I realized how much I had discovered about the human heart in those few short years. It was here that I had learned about cruelty and weakness and suffering and unspeakable acts of madness. It was also here that I had experienced unsolicited kindness and friendship and forgiveness and that capacity for love that can go beyond all reasonable limits. I learned that in the gray, churning turmoil of human conduct there could be love—as constant and powerful as the movement of the earth, and as tender and delicate as a child's prayer. As long as there was a spark of decency, some fragile remnant of human kindness left in you, there might be someone to see it and nurture it and stand by you until you were whole again. All of that was in the world.

My mother lives alone now, surrounded by friends and visited often by her children and grandchildren. My father died suddenly in 1980. When he died, he had been sober for twenty-six years. To some measure, he was able to develop those special bonds with his grandchildren that he had never formed with his own sons and daughter. That was something of a reprieve for him, but it was not enough. In the final years of his life, he realized that we had all reached an understanding of the torment he had gone through, and though no one could give back to him the years to relive, we could grant absolution. Katy and I, and even Ron, each found our own way to forgive him. I know he understood that. What I don't know is if he ever forgave himself.

Walter Roers was born and raised in Minneapolis. He graduated from the University of Minnesota with a degree in psychology and served in the United States Navy. He has worked for the state of Minnesota for more than thirty years. Roers and his wife have three sons and a daughter. *The Pact* is his first book.

To Carrie,
With warmest
regards to a
great friend.
Best wishes
8/10/00

LAST HEAT